D0280679

SeaWAR

Book II of the
SeaBEAN Trilogy

SARAH HOLDING

Medina Publishing

Contents

Teddington School Library

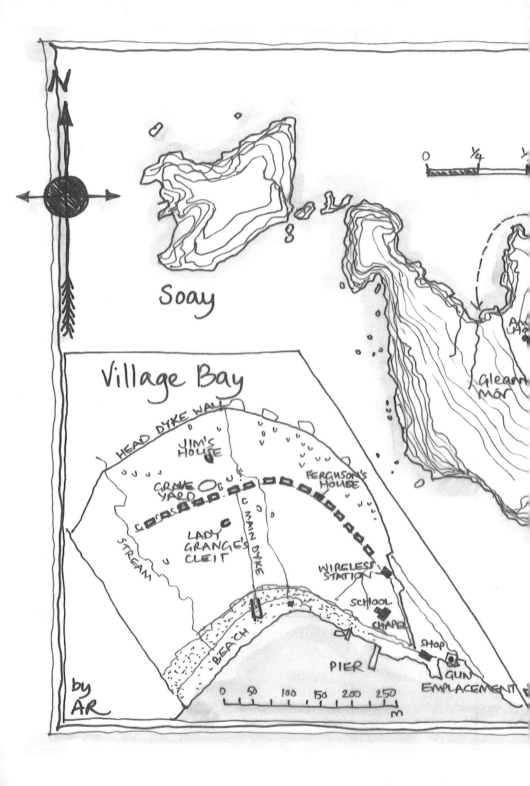

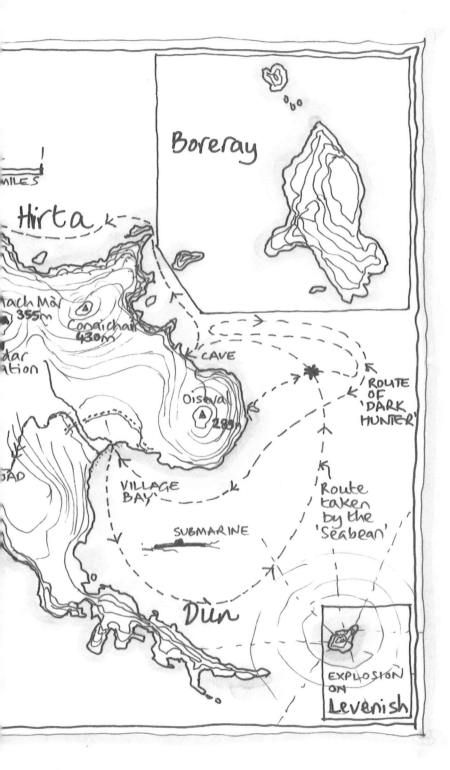

On a remote Hebridean airbase near Benbecula, a missile is launched. There have been many missiles tested from this location, but this is something new: it carries a nuclear bomb. Its target is a unique stack of rock called Levenish forty miles west, home to thousands of gannets and other seabirds, one of Scotland's sanctuaries. The missile hits the target and the stack is blasted to pieces on impact, shards of rock and bird raining down into the sea below.

A few hours afterwards, a military plane flies over the ocean to check on the damage the test nuclear warhead has caused. The RAF pilot steers a course through the billowing plume, catching occasional glimpses of the shattered rock below, not hearing the anguished cries of the remaining birds over the noise of his engine. He makes a few mental notes for his report, then smiles and tips the plane to turn back to base: the mission would appear to have been a success.

A few kilometres away, another man watches through binoculars from his post in a remote radar tracking station on the island of St Kilda. He makes a note of the time of the explosion and a small drawing of the sinister mushroom cloud in his brown leather notebook. Underneath the drawing in an urgent, rapid scrawl he writes:

THIS MOMENT IS A TURNING POINT THAT
CAN ONLY LEAD TO RUIN

Alice's Blog #1

1st May 2018, 8 am

Today is the day! The same helicopter that brought Granny and Gramps and my sister Lori over from the mainland when my baby brother Kit was born in January is coming to get the C-Bean off the rocks.

I should explain that our poor C-Bean Mark 3 is nearly dead. It's now just this pathetic abandoned cube wedged on the rocks at the end of our village on St Kilda, washed up there by the last storm. Or at least that's what all the grown-ups think. Looking at it now in that sorry state, no one would ever believe it's actually a mobile classroom, let alone a high-tech teleporting device with untold powers! Over the last few weeks we've watched it turn from a mysterious alien object like the blackest piece of outer space to a disgusting lump of junk covered in bird poo, barnacles and fish guts. Who would ever know it was once capable of transporting us kids from this remote Scottish island to anywhere in the world with just a single command?

It's probably a good job no one really knows – otherwise we would never have got away with such wild and dangerous adventures. It's only because they think it's teaching us things in a safe but exciting way that the adults ever agreed to get it airlifted off the rocks, because this whole rescue mission is awesomely expensive. Everyone around here thinks it got blown there during a very rough storm, but in actual fact it was due to a slight error in our navigation when we were coming back from the other St Kilda in Australia. That was weeks ago.

8 pm

What can I say? It was like a scene from an old James Bond film – the helicopter just plucked the C-Bean from the rocks and held onto it like a giant seabird clinging to its prey. All six of St Kilda's schoolchildren, that's me, Charlie, Edie, Hannah and the two Sams, were watching anxiously from the beach. I don't include my sister Lori, because she's sixteen and still at school on the mainland until July. We wanted everyone to come and watch, but the adults said they were all too busy getting things ready for our annual May Day party. All, that is, except my friend Old Jim, who's ancient and a bit eccentric – the one who lives in an underground house made of earth at the end of the village. For some reason he took a keen interest in the rescue mission, and managed to hobble all the way down to the gun emplacement just near the village shop to watch things earnestly, while our little brown dog Spex, who's adopted Jim as his owner, ran around barking.

There was one other special person who came to watch – the C-Bean's designer, Karla Ingermann. She's flown over from Germany to help us get it going again. She seems a bit shy around the adults but adores my baby brother. Today she pushed him in his buggy all the way up the concrete road to video the C-Bean being rescued from the radar station up at the top.

The worst bit was when there was a loud ripping sound and the C-Bean lunged downwards. It skimmed the surface of the waves and swung out of control from side to side for a few seconds. Then the pilot managed to tilt the helicopter upwards and lurch away at a steep angle. He was aiming for the cluster of buildings just past the jetty. The best bit was how he managed to just clear the old stone storehouse by a hundred millimetres, before he lowered the C-Bean into the schoolyard right next to the chapel.

So it's been the best May Day ever. There was no school, and everyone was on holiday. We had this massive outdoor party – we set out chairs and tables and ate a feast with two lambs from the next-door island of Soay that we roasted on a spit. Then we lit a celebration bonfire. We do that every year to celebrate May Day as a tradition, but really, for us kids, this year's party was all about getting our C-Bean back. For the adults, I suppose it was more about the fact that out in the bay, for the first time ever, my dad and Charlie's dad have managed to get the new wave energy machines working to generate enough power to keep the whole of St Kilda and the rest of the Western Isles going all day, every day. I'm pleased for our dads because they've worked really hard, and it's making them both ill. They've got itchy skin and their hair is starting to fall out!

Oh and there's one other important thing I should mention – this year, May Day marks the day that St Kilda finally belongs to us! They've paid for it with the anonymous cheque we gave them from selling the gold nugget we found, and the money that I think Old Jim must have secretly given them, and now we've signed all the documents, and so that's it – it's ours!

To make it more special, the village committee decided to plant a tree. This is really something because there are no trees whatsoever on our island, so it will be St Kilda's first and only tree. But not for long – the plan is to plant one tree every year on May Day from now on, so when us kids are grown up there'll be like a whole forest! Edie and Hannah's dad went over to the mainland last week and chose a stubby little Scots pine, which they brought back on the ferry, and left it standing outside Mrs Butterfield's shop until this afternoon. Now it's been planted right in front of the vicar's house. Mr Butterfield made a special plaque for it. It says:

ST KILDA'S FIRST TREE

PLANTED ON THE FIRST DAY OF OUR INDEPENDENCE

MAY 1ST 2018

After we'd planted it, we all sang a hymn, and then our parrot Spix appeared out of nowhere, flew around in a circle over our heads and then landed in the tree squawking, 'Olá, olá!'. Everyone clapped and then Spix took a little bow.

Monday 14th May 2018

Karla's been running loads of tests on the C-Bean for almost two weeks now, but there's not been a flicker of life. She says all its systems were down. All the wonder seems to have gone out of it. And its door is still hanging half off its hinges. I can hardly believe now that we were transported all the way to New York, Brazil, Hong Kong and Australia in that sorry looking thing. It smells of seaweed and is going kind of rusty. You can see gaps now where the black coating has been joined together because there are crusts of this yellowy-brown stuff forming. I'm sure there's more of it appearing every day.

Now that my brother Kit is four months old, our lovely temporary teacher from America, Dr Foster, has gone back home, which is a bit of a shame because we all really liked him. My mum is back as our schoolteacher, which is OK except that now I've got to call her Mrs Robertson again and it feels weird. She let us look inside the C-Bean the day after it was rescued. Hannah was the most upset. She keeps doing all these mad drawings of forests and fairgrounds and foreign cities and loads of other beautiful other places she says are inside the C-Bean, but my mum has no idea what she's on about. As far as Mum knows, the walls have always been that dark and slimy and there never was a table that appeared in the middle of the C-Bean with amazing illuminated maps and images. The two Sams begged Mum to let them clean inside it, but Karla said not to do anything for the time being. She has at least ordered a new hinge mechanism for the broken door, which is on its way from Germany, and she's said that while she's waiting for it to arrive, she's got to wade through millions of lines of computer code, trying to figure out what's wrong with it.

I suppose I should say what she looks like. Karla is twenty-eight with short spiky red hair. She's a quiet, skinny sort of person with a freckly face and glasses with thick lenses that make her eyes look smaller than they really are. She never smiles, only ever wears black, and doesn't seem to want to talk to any of the other adults. And she sniffs a lot. On the first day she got here, Edie whispered to me at break-time, 'I don't trust her, she's fake'. But then Edie is always looking for the bad side to things. Sometimes I wonder if she really wants them to turn out wrong.

Karla asked Mum for permission to turn the little broom cupboard next to the schoolroom into her office, and now she works in there night and day, peering at the smallest, fastest, coolest, thinnest laptop Charlie says he has ever seen. He says it's made in Finland and doesn't need a power cable because the battery works on thermopower waves. I guess that's just another kind of wave energy. Charlie's just twelve, but he's a complete computer nerd so I'm sure he knows what he's talking about. All I know is, that thin black thing of Karla's makes our school iPads look really old-fashioned.

Mrs Butterfield says Karla only goes back to sleep in the guest room over the pub in the wee small hours when it's already getting light and Mrs Butterfield is sorting out the shop before opening time. She thinks that Karla must be allergic to something on St Kilda because she is always sniffing and sneezing and has bought nearly all the packets of tissues Mrs Butterfield had in stock.

It was 8 am on 15th May, half an hour before school was due to start, and Alice wandered down the village street with Spix, her bright blue parrot, stalking her all the way. A fine Scottish rain had been falling since first light. Alice was daydreaming about the C-Bean's door opening mysteriously that first day it arrived on the beach, and how it recorded everything about her, and even projected a holographic image of her that talked back in her voice, and how she only had to imagine something and it would magically appear a few seconds later in a small recess in the wall.

Alice found herself alone in the schoolyard. She walked round and round the C-Bean's ruined exterior, singing an old Gaelic sea shanty they'd just learned and trailing her hand over its bumpy surface. Still humming the tune, she stopped in front of the tiny door concealing the access panel. She pressed the door very gently, and after a moment or two she could see it was trying to force itself open. She ran her fingernail around the perimeter of the door to dislodge the rusty, salty substance and ease it open. The cardkey she'd found in the sand on the beach on the first day was still in the slot. Alice closed her eyes and ran her fingers gently over the keypad inside, humming softly to herself. The buttons felt cold. She breathed warm air on them, talking under her breath, 'Come on C-Bean, you can do it. Remember me, Alice. Your friend?'

She opened her eyes a crack and thought she was imagining it at first. Was one of the lights on the panel glowing faintly? She breathed onto the keys again. They were warm to her touch now, and seemed softer somehow, like skin. She hummed a line from the song again, like a lullaby, and very slowly the row of lights starting pulsing red and green in sequence. Alice smiled a secret smile, and kept singing to the C-Bean, coaxing it back to life. After a few minutes it was humming the same pattern of notes back to her, very softly, but definitely making its own sounds. She wanted to run into the office and tell Karla, but she didn't dare leave the C-Bean at this critical moment of its recovery. She didn't want to call for her to come, either, in case the sound of shouting upset the C-Bean, so she stayed by its side until she could see Charlie in the distance leaping across the dykes, taking a shortcut to school. She beckoned wildly to him.

'Charlie, go and get Karla, tell her something's happening,' Alice said breathlessly when he was close enough to hear.

Karla immediately made a conference call to Germany from her tiny office. As the rest of the children arrived for school, they caught snippets of the conversation but none of them could understand any of it. All they knew was that Karla seemed very excited and kept sneezing and repeating the words '*biomimetische Funktion*'. After she ended the mobile phone call, Karla came into the classroom and told Mrs Robertson that some rather experimental things got added to the design of the C-Bean during its production process.

'I see. Why was that?' asked Alice's mother, putting six ticks in her register.

'It was in order to get around a few … malfunctions it had defeloped,' Karla admitted, and sneezed loudly.

The Sams started giggling because of her accent. Hannah, meanwhile, was drawing a picture of Karla on her iPad, and Edie was sitting with her arms folded, looking suspicious as usual.

'What kind of experimental things, Karla?' asked Charlie.

'Exactly as Alice found out just now – it responds to human warmth and touch and soothing sounds. Who thought it vood be possible?' Karla seemed completely amazed, and it made her accent stronger and more difficult to understand, perhaps because she was thinking too much in German.

'I knew about that the first time I found the C-Bean,' murmured Alice, almost to herself.

Alice was sent to get more tissues for Karla from the shop. When she came back, she couldn't resist loitering for a while by the C-Bean in the schoolyard.

'You can do it,' she breathed, her face very close to one of its walls. She touched one of the ridges of rust. To her amazement, it started to shrink very gradually under her fingertips. She worked her way slowly round all four sides until the rust had all but vanished. Then she eased the broken door open until there was a wide enough gap to slip through, took a deep breath and stepped inside.

There was a strong slimy fishy smell, like a pair of wellington boots that have been left with seawater inside. Every surface inside was still grimy and mouldy. Alice stood in the middle of the C-Bean with her eyes closed and focused her thoughts on the cleanest white bed sheets she'd ever seen, until she could picture them blowing and billowing in the wild St Kilda wind and could smell the sharp fresh air. After a while she didn't need to imagine the clean smell – she just knew the C-Bean was producing it itself, completely blotting out the fishy smell, and it had added in the sounds of the waves and seabirds to complete the atmosphere. When Alice opened her eyes again, the walls were clean, bright and alive. She was surrounded by a kaleidoscope of images from all over the island. It was as if the C-Bean was happy to be home and was busily sorting through its memory bank. Alice clapped her hands with joy, and ran out to get Karla.

By the time everyone trooped inside the C-Bean, including Spix, it was replaying moving images of the rescue mission, a silent witness to its own sea adventure. The children could see Old Jim in his ragged black clothes watching, as well as a colourful bunch of children shouting and waving down on the beach, right up until the cable started to break and it almost dropped into the sea. Curiously, as the C-Bean got to the part when it landed in the schoolyard, Alice realised that the movie had been filmed from where Karla had been standing, up by the radar station.

'Look, it's us!' chorused the Sams in unison.

Then the walls went blank again. Spix squawked loudly, as if in protest.

'Hmm, not quite fixed, then,' Edie couldn't resist saying.

'Oh come on, Edie. It was quite traumatic for the C-Bean, nearly getting dropped like that,' ventured Alice. Disappointed, the other children drifted back to class, but Alice stayed, her curiosity working overtime.

Karla went back to the office and brought out her shoulder bag containing her laptop. She sat down cross-legged on the floor of the C-Bean, scrolling through dense lines of computer code, looking for something in particular. Spix was fidgeting around on the floor, taking sunflower seeds from Alice's hand. Charlie was sent back to fetch Alice.

'Hey, your mum says you can't spend all day in here.'

Just then, the C-Bean started making a low crackling sound and the same complicated code – masses and masses of black symbols and numbers containing secret instructions – began moving up the walls around them. Suddenly one line appeared near the floor, highlighted in bright yellow. The C-Bean locked onto that one piece of information and then began duplicating the single line of code so it appeared on every surface, getting larger and larger. They all stared in amazement.

Reset

'Look!' said Charlie, 'it's worked it out for you, Karla. That's where the problem is.'

Karla looked up and smiled for the first time ever. When she glanced back at her laptop, the same line of code on her screen had been highlighted, and it appeared the C-Bean was busy making alterations by itself. The code was changing before her very eyes, without her needing even to touch the keyboard.

'Charlie, can you be a kind one and go back to my office and get my mobile phone? I again must call the guys in Germany, right this moment!'

Charlie went off to get it, and Alice started singing her song again, happy in the knowledge that the C-Bean might actually work. She could feel the wind picking up outside, coming down off the highest mountain, Conachair, into Village Bay to meet the incoming waves. It whistled round the schoolyard, as if it too was as impatient and excited as Alice felt. A sudden gust whipped up against the broken door and banged it shut. Spix let out a loud squawk. A shudder ran through the C-Bean's structure, and the walls went dark.

Karla sniffed loudly and then cleared her throat in the dimness. Alice could still see her face because of the glow from the laptop screen.

'Alice, can you please to check the door for me?' There was a tiny note of panic in her voice. She started rummaging in her bag for a tissue.

There was a thin line of daylight visible along one side where the door didn't fit properly anymore. Alice started to crawl towards it on her hands and knees. She experienced her own moment of panic then, when she realised the last time she'd crawled across the C-Bean like this was when it got stuck on the rocks coming back from Australia and she'd banged her head badly. She was just about to reach out for the door when the C-Bean started shivering. Soon the whole thing was vibrating and quivering. Karla's laptop slid off her lap and across the floor, then crashed into the wall opposite and stopped working. Alice stood up carefully in the dark and tried to push the door open, but it was stuck fast. They were trapped inside, unless Charlie could get it open again from the outside.

It was not easy trying to think with the C-Bean shaking so much. Alice sat on the floor and tried to calm it down, making 'shhh, shhh' sounds like she used to soothe her baby brother Kit. The movement of the C-Bean was making her feel quite nauseous. She could hear Karla muttering as she tried to get her laptop to reboot. Alice closed her eyes. There was another high-pitched scratchy noise building up from somewhere, like an old radio or TV that wasn't tuned in properly, something Alice's dad called white noise. It crackled and buzzed louder and louder. Karla started pummelling the walls with her fists and calling out.

'Charlie, Charlie, we're stuck! Help!' She paused, then blurted out, 'Alice, we are going to need to do a factory reset, now, quickly!'

'OK. But how do we do that?' asked Alice, trying to remain calm.

'We reset the date und time. Sorry, but I get fery – how do you say it – *claustrophobic*. I don't like being in small confined spaces. It makes me panic.'

Alice imagined the word 'reset' in her mind. She concentrated on each letter individually, as if she was making a handwritten display card. As she visualised the 't' at the end, a glowing white rectangle appeared out of the gloom on one wall of the C-Bean. At the left end of the white rectangle was a single vertical line, a cursor that blinked on and off. Karla stared in amazement.

'It wants us to input something,' she said impatiently. 'But what?'

Alice thought for a moment and then looked at her watch. She uttered a string of numbers, barely audible over the white noise.

'15-05-18, 08.45.'

The numbers appeared dutifully one by one behind the blinking cursor, and then paused. The C-Bean had steadied itself, and was now just rocking slightly to and fro. They both stared at the digits and waited. Nothing happened.

'It isn't working!' wailed Karla.

'Oh,' said Alice, realising her mistake. 'Reset.'

There was a sharp jolt and the C-Bean's door flew open. The pod's interior was suddenly flooded with sunlight, and they both squinted. Karla stood up and exhaled slowly, like she'd been holding her breath the whole time it had been wedged shut, and then ran out of the door, clutching her laptop and her bag. Spix rearranged his tail feathers and followed her. Alice stood in the doorway, her eyes still adjusting to the brightness.

What with the wind and all the shuddering and quivering, the C-Bean had moved quite a long way from the schoolyard and was now down by the shoreline facing the water, in almost the same place where it had been nearly dropped in the sea by the helicopter. The waves were breaking a few metres from the base of the pod. Alice groaned as she realised another winching was going to be necessary. However, miraculously, the problem with the door seemed to have been rectified – she found she could now click it shut behind her with no problem. She was just wondering how they would afford to move it all over again, when Karla came running back.

'Where are we?' she cried, looking confused and somewhat stricken. Alice thought the claustrophobia must have still been affecting her.

'On St Kilda,' Alice said gently as she looked around her.

There was something odd, for sure. She counted the houses in the village and found that there were six missing. The Scots pine wasn't there. Above the village, there was no concrete road winding up to the radar station on the ridge, just a dirt track. Nor was there a gun emplacement on the headland. And when she turned and looked out to sea, she couldn't see the wave energy station, either. Some things were where they should be, though – the school, the chapel, the little walled graveyard and, further up the slope, she could still make out the entrance to Old Jim's underground house.

'Erm. Let's go up to the schoolhouse and find the others,' Alice suggested.

They started to trudge up the beach towards the school and the chapel.

As they got nearer, a bell started ringing. A handful of children ran out of the classroom into the yard. Alice waved. But her classmates looked very unfamiliar somehow. They had all dressed up in olden-days clothes – the girls were wearing white smocks over brown dresses, and the boys wore britches and caps and hand-knitted woollen sweaters. Then it occurred to Alice that it wasn't their clothing that made them seem unfamiliar – these were not the St Kildan children she knew. She studied their faces. No Edie, Hannah, Charlie or a Sam among them. She stopped walking and stood still.

'Vat is wrong?' Karla asked.

'I'm not sure,' said Alice. 'But I think resetting the C-Bean has altered the clock a bit too much.'

One of the boys caught sight of Alice and Karla and called to the other kids. They stood in a line by the schoolyard wall and watched, pointing and whispering to each other as Alice approached, feeling somewhat shy. She was suddenly ver y conscious of her own clothes – jeans, a stripy rainbow-coloured fleece, and wellington boots with a yellow daisy pattern. And then there was her bright blue parrot, which hopped and fluttered along beside her.

'Hi. I'm Alice, I … live here,' she said brightly when she got close enough to talk without shouting over the sound of the wind.

Their spokesperson said, 'Good morning, miss. I'm Donald Ferguson. I've always lived here. You don't look as if you come from these parts.'

'Hello, Donald. This is my friend Karla, and this is my parrot, Spix,' continued Alice, trying to ignore the last remark. 'Can we speak to your teacher?'

'Aye, she's inside. It's ma mother. You can call her Dora.'

Alice smiled. At least one thing was familiar – having a mother for a teacher was definitely something she knew all about.

'Can I just check something out with you before we speak to … Dora?'

'Aye, mebbe,' Donald cocked his head on one side, curious.

'What's today's date?'

'I know, I know!!' All seven children put their hands up eagerly, wanting to answer Alice's question.

'Well?'

'Fifteenth of May, nineteen eighteen!' they chorused triumphantly.

✠ ✠ ✠

'A hundred years into the future, yes.' Alice said it for what felt like the hundredth time. It seemed very strange to be standing here in her own classroom, surrounded by the same cream walls and high ceiling, saying those words. She looked around her. Instead of an interactive whiteboard there were maps printed on curling, yellowing paper hanging on the walls. The children sat in two rows in stunned silence, staring first at Alice, then at Spix, then at Karla. In front of each of them were a slate and a piece of chalk instead of an iPad. Mrs Dora Ferguson, their teacher, was obviously in a state of shock, because she kept rubbing her hands together in an endless washing motion and pushing imaginary strands of hair back into the neat little bun on the back of her head. Finally, she turned to the blackboard behind her, picked up a piece of chalk, and slowly wrote the number 2018 on the board in large curling numerals. She gazed at it longingly for a while and then turned back to face Alice with a look of awe on her face.

'But how can that be?' she asked. 'How did you get here?'

'In something called a C-Bean. It was given to us earlier this year as an extra classroom, but it turned out to have special powers. I didn't know about this one until just now. It's never travelled back in time before,' Alice said matter-of-factly.

'A seabean, you say? Like the ones that get washed up on the beaches here sometimes.'

Alice smiled, remembering her own mysterious little seedpods – a Mary's bean and a hamburger bean.

'Well, it's a lot bigger than any of those, and it's shaped like a cube. You can come and see it if you like – it's down on the beach right now.'

'I see. And your friend … who is she?' Dora asked tentatively.

Karla had not said a word since they'd arrived at the school, and was standing rigidly by the door, clutching her shoulder bag in front of her as if for protection.

'Oh, this is Karla – she's the C-Bean's designer. She's from Germany,' Alice said cheerfully by way of introduction.

There was a gasp from several of the children, and Alice could hear them whispering 'She's a German!' to each other. Dora looked at Karla with a very grave expression.

'Oh, that is not good. Whatever are we going to do now?' She sat down heavily in the chair behind the teacher's desk and rested her head in her hands.

Alice turned to Karla. Claustrophobia suddenly seemed to be the least of her worries. The children were fiddling with their inkwells, fidgeting and squirming in their seats.

Dora looked up suddenly and asked them to file outside. They obeyed her at once, trooping out in a line, heads down.

With her pupils gone, the teacher tried to compose herself. She leaned forward and ran her hands over the old-fashioned wooden desk in front of her, as if she was feeling for some tiny lost item. She smiled politely, stood up and cleared her throat.

'You must realise, surely, that we are in the middle of a war. It might not seem like it on this remote island, but we have been at war for the past four years. Do they not teach you about this war in the future? So many people have been killed. We don't know when it's ever going to end. The Germans just won't give up.'

Dora looked accusingly at Karla as she started pacing up and down the aisle between the two rows of desks, darting anxious glances out of the window at the C-Bean. From here it looked like an ominous black tombstone standing on the foreshore.

Alice suddenly remembered the commemorative plaques inside the chapel, listing all the men who'd died in the First and Second World Wars. She murmured an inscription to herself: 'First World War, 1914–1918'.

'What did you say?' asked Dora, wheeling round and fixing Alice with a stare.

Alice was about to repeat what she'd said, but there were two things that occurred to her in that moment. One good – she could tell Dora this war was going to end soon – this year even; and one bad, that it was going to be followed by an even more horrible war against the German Nazis – the Second World War.

Instead she said quietly, 'I know a bit about the war, yes'.

'And your friend?'

'Karla knows too. It was a long time ago, and Germany and Britain are friends now.'

'Is that so?' Dora said slowly, mulling over this new information. 'But we are going to have to keep this very hush-hush for now. I mean, the people on this island are very nervous and suspicious because of the war effort, and they will naturally think that Karla is some kind of spy.'

Alice found the notion quite exciting, but decided not to say anything. Karla just looked tired and embarrassed. She had slumped into a chair by the door. She didn't look anything like a spy, Alice thought, feeling quite sorry for her.

'Alice, I think that in the circumstances it would be best if you and Karla and your parrot were to go home right now in your time-travel machine, and never come back.'

Something in the way Dora said this made Alice realise it was actually the last thing the teacher wanted to happen. Although she was afraid, she was also curious and wanted to learn more, as any good teacher would.

Alice looked at Karla, who shrugged. Then Dora had another idea.

'Your seabean – can you make it invisible?'

'I don't think so, although …' Alice said slowly, remembering that it could produce objects that would then disappear once you took them outside the C-Bean.

'I read about this magician in London who can make things invisible by throwing a cloak over them, so there must be a way,' Dora insisted.

'Why don't you come and see it for yourself?' Alice suggested. The children were jostling each other impatiently outside the door now, waiting to be called back inside.

Dora hesitated, and then without a word she removed the apron she was wearing, hung it tidily over the back of her chair and reached her overcoat down from the peg beside the blackboard.

She opened the door and made an announcement.

'Children, we are going for a walk to see something of great interest, and nobody is to misbehave. Do you understand?'

As they walked past the chapel, Alice looked in through the open door. The wall where the plaques should be was empty. Donald came up beside her. They were the same height. He had an earnest look in his brown eyes that reminded her of someone, but she couldn't think who it was.

'You're aliens.'

'I suppose we must seem like that. But I can assure you we're not from another planet.'

'Have you read *The Time Machine* by Jules Verne?'

'No, but I've heard of it,' Alice answered.

Donald was a bit out of breath as he jogged along beside Alice, who was, out of habit, counting her footsteps and only half listening.

'It's about a man – the Time Traveller,' Donald continued, 'and he builds a machine that lets him go to the future. Is that what you are – a time traveller?'

He stumbled on by Alice's side waiting for an answer. They were almost back at the C-Bean.

'*Olá!*' Spix got there first and triumphantly announced his arrival, which made all the children laugh.

'A hundred and sixty-seven,' Alice said out loud when she took the final step and stood in front of the C-Bean.

'I thought so,' said Donald, as if her bizarre answer proved it.

The children fell silent as they stepped inside the C-Bean. Even Donald, who'd been talking non-stop all the way down the hill, was now dumbstruck by the tiny, empty interior. After a while, he couldn't contain himself any longer and a torrent of questions poured out.

'Where are all the buttons and dials? Where's the clock to tell it what year to visit next? How do you control it? Where do you sit? Why is it all dark and empty? Is it powered by steam or coal?'

Alice was unsure of some of the answers. She wanted to show them what it could do, but she also felt shy and protective of the C-Bean's incredible powers. So it was Karla who spoke for the first time.

'The C-Bean is an adfanced piece of Western technology, that uses biomimetic micro-electronic self-organising systems to orientate itself and learn about the enfironments it finds itself in. These unique attributes make it an ideal learning enfironment, and so we – *wie sagt man auf Englisch* – adapted its original use for the education market early in 2116. I mean in 2016 …'

Karla's voice droned on like a voice-over from a science documentary. The children were all open-mouthed now. Even to Alice she sounded like a strange alien intelligence from a distant future.

'I don't know what all that means, either,' said Alice, as if reading their minds, 'but I want to show you something. Watch this.'

Alice began, softly at first, to sing the words of the old Gaelic sea shanty that had made the C-Bean come back to life, and soon it was displaying all over its four walls moving images of old wooden fishing boats being tossed at sea, huge nets being hauled in, piles of silvery fish heaped up on jetties, and women in headscarves gutting them and throwing them into buckets. The children, their eyes wide as they watched the scenes playing out all around them, also knew the song and started to join in, shyly at first; then Dora began to sing too in a high, strained voice and their voices grew louder, until they were all singing heartily.

The C-Bean, bolstered by their lively sing-song, embarked on an ambitious imaginary sea voyage, the wind blowing freely, sails flapping, and up in the clear blue sky overhead seabirds were wheeling and diving. Alice smiled as she noticed Spix trying to copy them by flying around in the confined space. She was remembering the time she and Edie found themselves out in Village

Bay because Dr Foster had got the coordinates for St Kilda ever so slightly wrong. Just like that time, there was a slight lurching movement beginning, and a certain mistiness gathering in the waves around them, as if the walls were becoming a little bit porous …

Alice noticed that Karla was the only one not singing. Instead she had pulled a tiny camera out of her shoulder bag and was photographing everything that was happening in the C-Bean with a serious look on her face. Alice thought Karla was probably feeling claustrophobic again – even though the C-Bean was producing lots of outdoor images, they were still in a confined space. So Alice stopped singing, and the sea voyage subsided, along with the lurching motion. The mist cleared and the walls hardened over.

The children uttered a disappointed 'ohhh!' in unison and Dora, shaking her head in disbelief, laughed and said, 'Yes, I think that's enough now'. But Donald was persistent.

'What else can it do? Let's go somewhere real and get out and look around, like you did, Alice!' The other children looked terrified and excited in equal measure at their classmate's suggestion. Donald tried again.

'Mrs Ferguson, what about going to see that Crystal Palace down in London you were telling us about yesterday? You know, in Hyde Park where they had the Great Exhibition in 1851? We could go there! I mean *then!*'

'Well, Donald, I don't think that's such a good idea. We might get stuck there and be unable to get back. Alice – is that a possibility?'

'We've always got home before,' Alice said truthfully.

'Let's at least try. Please!' Donald urged.

There was an eager, fidgety silence among the children. Dora smoothed her hair and chewed her lip, and made more washing motions with her hands. Then she buttoned up her coat and said, 'All right, Alice, can you take us there? It would be extremely interesting, I have to admit. I've never even been to London before.'

Alice smiled and said, 'Neither have I'.

Alice requested a pen, and the children gasped when one just appeared as if by magic in a recess in the wall of the C-Bean. Then she called up the geographical coordinates for Hyde Park, London, and using the pen wrote the date and time very precisely, this time including the century – 15/05/1851, 09.30 – and their destination on the white wall behind her. The children were sitting on the floor watching her every move. Karla was filming the whole thing.

'Don't forget about making it invisible,' Dora reminded Alice; and so to please her, Alice added the word 'invisible' after the date, and underlined it twice, even though she had no idea if it would work.

As she did so, it suddenly occurred to Alice that here she was, just a few months after she'd found herself accidentally in New York's Central Park with her 2018 classmates and their teacher Dr Foster, trying – this time on purpose – to transport the C-Bean from St Kilda to London's Hyde Park with a group of schoolchildren from 1918, to a time even longer ago – one hundred and sixty-seven years, to be precise.

✠ ✠ ✠

There was the slightest of jolts, and then the door clicked open. The C-Bean had landed on a long red carpet, and Alice thought for a moment that somehow the Victorians knew they were due to arrive from the future, and had rolled out the carpet specially. But as it turned out, the C-Bean had simply landed awkwardly on the spot where two main routes crossed.

There was a steady hum of excited voices. It felt stiflingly hot. Spix, who had been perched on Alice's shoulder, suddenly let go and whirled up into the space above their heads. Alice looked up and gasped. They were inside an enormous greenhouse with a very high glass roof. All around her were gleaming Victorian inventions, some with steam pouring out of them. Hundreds of people were milling about between them, the women all wearing bonnets and long dresses, the men in long-tailed coats with top hats. Huge colourful flags and drapes were hanging down from an upper level. Alice could vaguely remember a biscuit tin at her Granny's house with a picture on it that looked very similar. She turned round to look at the C-Bean, to try to imagine what people in 1851 would make of this dark and mysterious invention from the future. But the C-Bean wasn't there!

Alice had a momentary panic until she realised that the 'invisible' command must have worked. She stretched out her hands. The ends of her fingers made contact with its velvetty outer surface, even though she couldn't see it. She realised they were going to have to remember this exact spot if they went off exploring and wanted to find it again. Alice surveyed her surroundings more carefully. There was a vast green combustion engine to their left and some sort of golden oriental pagoda to their right.

Dora had the children grouped around her skirts and was pointing things out and explaining what they were. Alice thought the teacher had a sparkle in her eye that hadn't been there before. One of the children, a little girl of about seven or eight with rosy cheeks, came up to her and held her hand. Alice could see that Donald was itching to explore, whereas Karla seemed reluctant to leave the C-Bean. She stood in her black jeans and black leather jacket, clutching her shoulder bag with one hand and blowing her nose nervously with the other. Alice thought she looked as if she wished she, too, were invisible like the C-Bean.

Donald grabbed Alice's arm and asked, 'Have you ever seen a real tree before? Apparently there are three elm trees growing in here. I just overheard a man tell some people it's down that way,' he said, pointing. They set off down the red carpet, Spix swooping and squawking above their heads, the little girl still holding Alice's hand, with Dora and the others struggling to catch up. Donald was in the lead, ploughing a furrow through the crowds.

The elm trees were huge and very still. It seemed that the glasshouse must have been put up around them, because they were definitely growing in the ground. Alice and Donald walked round and round the biggest one in the middle. Spix settled happily on one of the branches. He kept crying 'Olá, olá!' which appeared to amuse the Victorian visitors, who were trying to catch a glimpse of Alice's exotic bird, assuming it was one of the exhibits. But Alice and Donald, coming as they did from an island with no trees to speak of, were more interested in the elms. A seedpod had fallen off one and landed on the red carpet. Alice picked it up and studied the hard nut in the centre surrounded by a delicate papery fringe, like the beige wings of a moth. She put it in her jeans pocket.

They wandered part way down another aisle, somewhat unsure of what to do next. 'I think it might be time to go back now,' said Dora, sensing that all the children, Alice included, were a little overwhelmed by the crowds and the heat. No one disagreed, and they all trooped back in the direction of the C-Bean. They could see Karla still standing awkwardly on the red carpet.

'It is a relief you are coming back,' she breathed when they got nearer. 'The infisibility function is starting to wear off – look!'

It was true – people were becoming aware of the C-Bean's presence, which was slowly turning into a golden mirrored surface. There were several ladies standing around it, adjusting their bonnets and expressing fascination at being able to see their own reflections in what seemed to be a huge mirror made of gold. Just then, a child accidentally ran into it. Where his forehead bumped the C-Bean, a patch of blackness started to appear.

Donald suddenly blurted out, 'Alice, they've called the police, look!'

Alice turned and saw two uniformed policemen in domed helmets marching towards them along the red carpet, waving truncheons. She remembered how they got into trouble with the police in New York for parking the C-Bean in Central Park without a permit. A look of terror flickered across Dora's face at the prospect of being arrested and detained by a Victorian police officer and, in an effort to prevent this from happening, Alice hurried everyone back inside the C-Bean, clicked the door shut and quickly barked out St Kilda's coordinates from memory.

A fter the usual jolt there was an expectant pause.

'How do we know if we're back?' Donald asked.

'We don't – we just open the door and find out,' said Alice matter-of-factly.

'Can we get outside quickly, because I feel ... how you say ... a bit sick,' Karla announced.

Alice opened the door. For some reason they had arrived up near Old Jim's underground house. Karla dropped her bag on the floor and ran out onto the hillside to be sick in the grass. Dora and the children hung back in the C-Bean, also a little stunned at what had just happened. Alice looked outside to see if the C-Bean had recovered its visibility. She was surprised to see that in one way it had and in another it hadn't. Its outer surface was now camouflaged to look like a very large stone enclosure or *cleit*, the kind that are dotted all over the island and in which the old St Kildans used to keep food and fuel dry over winter.

Alice chuckled to herself. 'That's very clever.'

'What's clever about that?' remarked Donald, scanning the scene in front of him. 'I don't think your time machine quite worked that time!'

Alice turned towards the village. She could hear the chapel bell ringing in the distance. She could make out a group of islanders entering the front door of the chapel. It looked smaller than before, until she realised there was no schoolroom built on the side. Along the main street half the houses were missing – all the ones with the tar-black roofs. Nor, she discovered to her dismay, was there a storehouse, a pier or a landing jetty. Things were getting into the habit of disappearing!

Dora stood on the threshold peering out, the other children pushing to try and get a look for themselves.

'It's not 1918, is it, Alice?' she said quietly.

Donald cleared his throat and announced firmly, 'Alice and I will go and investigate'.

'Please be careful, both of you, and come back as quickly as you can,' Dora sighed. She gazed up at the sky with a faraway look in her eyes. Seabirds were calling – it sounded like home, but it wasn't. The sound made Alice stop dead in her tracks. She suddenly realised Spix had not come back with them.

'Spix! We left Spix!'

Donald could see she was upset. He stood biting his lip with his arms hanging limply, anxious to explore but aware Alice needed some words of comfort.

'I'm so sorry, Alice. But you know, we left him in the best birdcage ever built – he'll love flying around there and entertaining everyone all day!'

'I suppose so,' Alice said, brightening a little at the thought. 'Poor Spix!'

She looked at her watch. It was gone 10 am. It occurred to her that Spix wasn't the only thing she was feeling anxious about. She had been missing from her own time well over an hour now – what must her mother be thinking? What must Charlie have told her mother when he realised that Alice and Karla had somehow got stuck in the C-Bean just as it was beginning to work again?

'Let's go this way to the chapel, Donald.'

Alice took a deep breath and started to follow the dyke that ran along above and behind the old turf-roof houses, so they wouldn't be noticed. There were sheets and clothes hanging out to dry in the backyards. A few chickens were pecking in the grass. As they got near, the last of the islanders were just entering the chapel – an old man with his arm around his wife, who was weeping into a handkerchief. The door closed softly behind them and the bell stopped ringing. Alice held her finger across her lips to tell Donald to stay silent, and they crept over the wall and went to stand under the window.

A service was just starting. It was all in Gaelic, but Donald could understand and was listening carefully. To Alice, it all sounded very sombre. There was a lot of intense talking in low voices, and when the congregation finally sang a hymn, it sounded more like wailing than singing. After a while, the bell started ringing again, a single plaintive note carried away on the sea breeze. The door of the chapel creaked open, and Donald and Alice moved swiftly round to the end of the building so that no one would see them. Donald seemed desperate to tell her something. He pointed for them to move further away, down to the shore.

'What is it?' Alice whispered as they hid behind some rocks.

'Not good,' announced Donald. 'It was a funeral. For a week-old baby.'

'Oh,' said Alice. 'How sad.'

They both fell silent for a moment and watched as a forlorn huddle of women formed outside the chapel and began talking amongst themselves. One of them cuddled another baby wrapped in several shawls. The men were still inside.

'They said it was the fifth newborn baby to die this year, and another is already sick. They were saying lots of prayers for them. Then there was a big discussion about whether they should all emigrate to Australia. Apparently there's going to be a chance to leave in the next few months on a ship. Some people want to, and others don't want to give up on their life here. They've got hardly any food. I know what that's like …' Donald bit his lip and looked unsure of himself for a moment.

'Go on,' said Alice softly.

'We had the same problem when I was little – we'd all been starving hungry for weeks, and we waited ages for them to send us emergency supplies from the mainland, but for our family it came too late. My Dad had already died.'

'Oh, you poor people!' Alice let out a heartfelt sigh. She remembered the vicar telling them just a few months ago at school about the babies in St Kilda who kept dying only days after they were born. They got ill because of some oil that was put on them that was meant to keep them healthy, but she couldn't remember the whole story. And the other thing – about Australia – she knew a bit about that too, how most of the people who left on the ship became ill and died on the way, only a few actually making it all the way to the other side of the world. But she didn't know about the islanders starving. Her stomach starting churning in sympathy, and she felt sorry for these hungry, helpless people. She forced back the tears by thinking hard.

'So,' she said at last, 'it must still be 1851, because I remember now that's the year before people left for Australia'.

'We should get back to your Seabean,' Donald nudged her elbow. 'I don't want to be sent to Australia!' He was trying to make a joke, and Alice smiled.

'You're right, Donald – that would be too weird. Let's go back.'

They ran back along behind the wall, stooping low and picking their way between the tussocks of rough grass still laden with dew. Alice glanced down into the graveyard and saw a freshly-dug oblong hole, the earth mounded up alongside. It was obviously for the baby. There were other new-looking graves, too, with little wooden crosses, where a child no bigger than a doll was buried.

Back in the C-Bean, Dora and the children were busy playing games it had generated to keep them amused – dominoes, chess and backgammon. The children were chattering away, engrossed in the novelty of moving the digital pieces around the C-Bean's white walls with their fingers and waiting for it to respond. Dora looked up.

'Well?'

'It's still 1851. We weren't clear enough about the time when we set off back – I'm not used to this function yet,' Alice said apologetically. 'Where's Karla?'

'She disappeared over the hill. I didn't dare call for her,' Dora said.

'Donald, can you go and find her?' Alice asked.

Alice noticed that the little girl who'd held her hand was playing outside the C-Bean with the pen it had produced to write the coordinates earlier. For some reason, it had not disappeared when it was taken out of the C-Bean this time. Alice wondered whether by resetting the C-Bean, it had changed the way the objects it produced behaved – instead of evaporating when they were taken outside, it seemed now that the things it made were permanent.

An idea formed in Alice's head.

'What's your name?' she asked the child.

'Elsa.'

'Elsa, may I have the pen, please?'

She took the pen back inside the C-Bean and began to write a list of items on one wall in large capital letters – oats, milk, eggs, sugar, butter, flour, carrots, cheese, apples, bananas, oranges, honey, bacon, potatoes, sausages. Then she smiled to herself, and as an afterthought added her favourite item of food – *ketchup*.

An opening appeared in the wall next to where she was standing, and there in the recess was a large wicker hamper piled high with all the things on the list, including a large bottle of tomato ketchup sticking out of the top. Alice lifted the hamper from the recess and started to drag it across the floor towards the door.

'Is that a picnic for our lunch?' Elsa asked, watching her closely.

'No, this isn't for you, sorry,' Alice said, as she manoeuvred the hamper out through the door.

Donald had found Karla and was walking back towards the C-Bean with her.

'What's all that for?' Donald asked.

'It's for the starving villagers. I want to leave them something before we go.'

'Good idea,' Donald remarked approvingly.

They each took a handle and carried the hamper across the grass and into the graveyard enclosure, where they put it down beside the open grave.

'Look! They're coming,' Karla called.

Alice and Donald both looked up, startled. They could see the villagers were moving in a slow procession up the main street towards the graveyard, four men at the front carrying a tiny coffin on their shoulders.

'Wait, there's one more thing I need to leave for them!'

Alice ran back to the C-Bean and scribbled something else on the wall – *medical kit*. She added out loud, 'For the babies! Please, quickly!'

A second later, the C-Bean produced a neat-looking green box with a white cross on top. Alice grabbed it and ran outside.

'It's too late, they've seen us!' Donald muttered.

Ignoring him, Alice darted into the graveyard and tucked the kit inside the basket with the food. She could hear the rustling of skirts and shuffling footsteps not far behind her, and a stern voice said something in Gaelic, which she imagined meant 'Who are you?' But Alice didn't turn to look this time. She just fled back to the C-Bean, her heart pounding in her mouth. She didn't want to have to explain she was from the future for a second time that day.

Alice was very clear with her instructions to the C-Bean this time, and spoke the date out loud as well as writing it on the wall. There was a brief but unnerving jolt that possibly signalled they had switched centuries – or so they hoped. Alice checked her watch – it was now almost 11 am, but was it 1918? And why hadn't the door opened?

They all stood, stiff and tense, waiting. Alice could just make out a man's voice speaking very slowly into a loudhailer, in an accent similar to Karla's. His words were muffled through the walls of the C-Bean, but it sounded like: 'You must take cover immediately. We intend to begin bombardment in five minutes.'

'What's going on out there?' Donald asked impatiently. 'Come on, I want to get out and see.'

They could hear people running and a panicked voice shouting, 'Where are the children? They're not in here!' Someone passed even closer and replied, 'They must have been captured. Come on, you heard what they said. We've got to get to safety.' Alice tried the door again, but it would not budge. She thought for a second, then commanded, 'Manual override!' – but still the C-Bean did not respond.

A few moments later there was a series of loud bangs. They were so ferocious it sounded like a building exploding. Alice could hear what sounded like rocks and stones coming crashing down, and then something large hit the top of the C-Bean, making the door fly open. A shard of timber blocked their exit, and the air outside was filled with dust. It was impossible to tell where they had arrived, but it was a place none of them wanted to be – there was more rapid firing, and each time something hit its target the noise was deafening. Dora shouted above the din that she didn't think anyone should venture forth – they were safer inside the C-Bean for the time being. The children had clustered around her, coughing and choking as the dust drifted into the C-Bean. All except Donald, who was standing alert and ready for action. There were brief pauses between the rounds of gunfire, and in one of these, he scurried out of the C-Bean, climbed through the rubble and disappeared into the dust cloud outside.

Alice was unsure what to do, but she felt responsible for landing them in this mess. Dora was trying her best to calm the bewildered children. She gave Alice and Karla a look that said, 'Do something!' There was another volley of shots, and their deadly echoes, followed by the sound of something else being destroyed further off. Then silence. Alice beckoned to Karla and turned towards the door to pick her way out of the C-Bean. She felt sure they must be in a large city where war was being waged, but which city and which war? Perhaps they were still in Hyde Park, but in 1918. The air was full of the smell of burning and gunpowder. But mixed in there was something familiar – a fresher, cleaner smell.

Alice groped her way forward and the dust cleared enough for her to see that she was standing in front of the shattered remains of a stone building. As she walked a bit further, she noticed there was grass underfoot, and the sound of waves breaking. When the dust cleared some more, Alice could see a familiar shoreline stretching out in front of her that confirmed they had arrived back home in St Kilda. But there was no sign of Donald, and the whole place looked battered and deserted. All around buildings spewed forth flames and black smoke. One house was almost completely destroyed. The clean fresh smell was the sea. Alice stared out into the bay. There was a dark shape moving slowly underwater, a whale of some kind perhaps. It was slowly submerging and retreating.

She heard a noise behind her and turned abruptly. A boy in school uniform was running towards her, covered in dust with blood running down his forehead. As he came closer, she realised it was Donald.

'Did you see, did you see? It's a German U-boat – I mean submarine – look, Alice! I reckon it's run out of ammunition now!' He sounded strangely excited – as if he had waited a long time for something this real to happen that would make him believe once and for all that his country was truly at war.

'How did you get hurt?' Alice asked, and asked Karla for a tissue to wipe away the blood.

'I'm fine, leave it,' Donald mumbled, pushing Karla away, his eyes trained on the horizon. Karla put the tissues back in her bag and took out her camera. She started taking photographs of the German submarine. They watched it turn and leave the bay to go round the headland.

'You can see its periscope!' Donald spluttered as it withdrew beneath the waves. Karla turned the camera inland, and began photographing all the damage.

Alice and Donald surveyed the wreckage too.

'They've decimated the storehouse, look! And the wireless station!'

It appeared the commander of the German submarine must have also been suspicious of the stone cleitean dotted around the bay, because a lot of them had been blown to smithereens.

Karla suddenly blurted out in a panic, 'The C-Bean, where is it gone?'

All three of them ran back to the schoolyard and, seeing Dora and the children emerging seemingly out of thin air, realised that it must still be there. Karla moved towards them.

'It's just being infisible again. I can feel it.'

But Alice realised there was no way of knowing if their invisible time machine was damaged or not. She could only hope it had been in some way protected by the surrounding buildings.

There was an eerie silence on the island, partly because there was no wind. Alice turned to speak to Donald. He was shaking violently. She remembered seeing a film about the Gulf War once, and her mum had explained to her that soldiers often behave strangely when they are in a state of shock.

'Where do you think they all went to take cover, Donald?' she asked gently.

'Over there somewhere, maybe in one of the ditches,' he said, jerking his thumb backwards over his shoulder but unable to turn and look in that direction. Alice scanned the area beyond the village. There was no one in sight.

'I'm sure they're all safe, wherever they are,' she said.

Donald suddenly turned and ran in that direction.

Alice watched Donald stumbling along the village street and then diving into what must have been his own house about halfway up.

'Alice! Karla! What's happening? Is Donald hurt?' Dora called out anxiously from the C-Bean.

'As far as we can tell, the island has been attacked by a German submarine,' Alice reported. 'But it's gone now, and I think it's safe to come out. Donald's hurt his head and he's a bit shaken up. I think he's gone home.'

Dora picked her way carefully over the rubble, and turned to help her pupils clamber out. She looked around at the scene of devastation and her hands started making washing motions again without her realising. They all stood in a quiet huddle.

'We were so undefended. I suppose this was always going to happen, but why now?' she asked of no one in particular. 'Look at the mess! How are we ever going to get straight again?'

A tear rolled down one cheek and she brushed it away. 'Just so long as no one was …'

But she couldn't bring herself to finish the sentence.

'Donald thinks they are all hiding in a ditch.'

'I sincerely hope so. I must return the children to their parents.' Dora put her hand over her mouth, unsure whether to say sorry, thank you or both to Alice, who had a very forlorn look on her face. Karla surveyed the scene blankly through her thick glasses and started shivering.

'Come with us, Alice – you too, Karla. We all need to get over the shock.'

'Are you sure? Maybe it would be better if we didn't – there are some things we can't possibly explain.'

Before they could make a decision, Alice spotted two men in uniform walking briskly towards them, one of them armed.

'Take the children to safety, Mrs Ferguson,' said one of the men. 'You're safe now – we'll take care of things from here.'

The man gestured with his gun for them to go. Dora nodded, shepherding her charges in front of her and beckoning to Alice. Alice grabbed Karla's hand and started to go with them.

'Not you,' the man said gruffly, lifting his arm and barring her way with the gun. Alice stood rooted to the spot, feeling the weapon against her throat.

'The two foreigners come with us,' the other man said, pointing at Karla and Alice.

Alice's Blog #2

16th May 1918

I've persuaded them to let me have some paper and a pencil. Maybe there's a chance that someone will find what I've written, but the main thing is I have to record everything that happens to me here, otherwise I'm worried I'll lose track of time. We've been gone over 24 hours now. What must Mum and Dad be thinking?

Karla is in the same situation as me, only it's more serious for her, because she really is an enemy: not only has she admitted she's a German, but she also had some very strange futuristic items in her shoulder bag such as her laptop and her camera, which have of course been confiscated. That made her really grumpy, and now she frowns all the time and mumbles a lot in German.

With me, they're just not sure. No matter how much Dora has reassured them I'm just an ordinary eleven-year-old Scottish schoolgirl, they won't believe it because they think I must have brainwashed her into saying that. As far as they're concerned I also represent some kind of unknown threat, because I don't speak Gaelic, I am wearing strange clothes, I don't have any identity papers and I seem to have mysteriously arrived from nowhere. All of which is, of course, true.

I've heard about prisoners of war, or PoWs, but I've never really thought about what it meant before. I am sure there aren't many prisoners who are kept locked up all day in a damp stone cleit like this one and have to sleep on straw mattresses at night, which are very itchy. Donald and Dora are allowed to visit us, and brought us oatcakes Dora made for us. Karla is really struggling in here because of her claustrophobia. She says she doesn't mind the dark, it's the fact that it's a confined space and she feels trapped. She says she wants to escape, but there's someone outside the entrance to the cleit guarding us at all times.

He tried to scare us last night by telling us that this particular cleit is haunted by someone from centuries ago called Lady Grange. I thought he was just winding us up, but when I asked Donald about it, he said it's true, there was a woman called Lady Grange who was once imprisoned in this very hovel. Someone quite posh, but a bit feisty, from Edinburgh. Her mean old husband wanted to get rid of her apparently, and smuggled her here against her will. It's all a bit spooky. This morning Donald brought me a book about her that he found in the schoolroom. It said that in all the thirty years she was a prisoner here she was only allowed to write three letters, and that only one of those ever made it to the mainland. Just before she was about to be rescued by the person who got that letter, her guards took her to the Isle of Skye, where she died. The story keeps going round and round in my head. I must be going a bit crazy because I thought I could hear Lady Grange crying – until I realised it was Karla.

She won't admit it, but I've heard her. Her eyes were all puffy this morning behind her glasses. It made me feel really homesick because all I could think about was my brother Kit crying for a feed in the night, and then I got really upset. Last night Karla was talking in her sleep. I thought I was dreaming, because she kept saying 'Kit, I'm sorry, but the mission is a failure. We have to go to Plan B.' Except that she pronounced B as 'bay'. I know she's fond of my baby brother, but it was still weird that she should be talking in English to him like that in her sleep.

When we were eating breakfast this morning I said to her, 'Karla, what's Plan Bay?' She looked kind of embarrassed, as if I had found something out I shouldn't have. She told me her company had made her sign something called a 'confidentiality agreement' when she started working for them, so she was 'not at liberty to say'. Donald tells me he'd heard that she said the exact same thing to the army officers when they took her off for questioning yesterday. So I told her she needed to be a bit less secretive, or she will never be allowed out of this place. It was meant as a piece of helpful advice, but she took it the wrong way. Now she won't talk to me at all. I can still hear her sniffing in the darkness, though.

17th May 1918

Karla has vanished! Whoever was guarding us during the night must have fallen asleep, because when I woke up this morning, she had gone. Donald came to see me before school, and told me they've mounted a search party to look all over the island for her. But I'm more worried that she will go back to the C-Bean and somehow make it take her back to 2018 without me. So I have been trying to send the C-Bean urgent messages in my head not to let her control it.

Donald says that the C-Bean is still there, but people have started noticing something strange, because although it's managing to remain invisible most of the time, occasionally there is a flicker when it's suddenly visible for a moment or two and you can see this weird black shape appearing.

He managed to hand me a note without the guard noticing. I waited until after they took my breakfast tray away before I opened it. Donald's obviously also been worrying about Karla taking the C-Bean and leaving without me, so he's come up with his own Plan B, and is going to come and get me later to help me get home. They're holding a big meeting this morning in the chapel to decide what to do about me, and about recapturing Karla. Donald says he's stolen some sleeping potion from his mum's medicine cabinet and slipped it into the guard's tea flask, so later this morning, when it's taken effect, Donald's going to rescue me.

D onald was hiding behind the wall in the graveyard. He had been watching the guard taking slurps from his flask since about 8 am, and when he saw him slump sideways in the doorway just before 10 am, he ran across to the cleit and whispered into the dark interior.

'Alice, it's time.'

They half walked, half ran down the village street towards the chapel. They both knew they would have to remain absolutely silent, since the C-Bean was standing right beside the building where the whole village was assembled to determine Alice's fate. They crept round the back of the chapel and into the yard. It looked empty. Alice's heart was thumping. What if the C-Bean had already gone? She groped around until she ran into one smooth wall, and heaved a sigh of relief. She worked her way round the sides until she had located the access panel and popped it open. Her stomach lurched when she could feel that the cardkey was missing from its slot. She knew instinctively that Karla must have taken it, and had no idea if the C-Bean would work without it. Donald watched as she ran her hand over the keypad to warm the keys, but the tiny lights did not come on. Alice didn't dare sing the sea shanty out loud, but instead started coaxing the C-Bean under her breath, until eventually the door clicked open. Donald and Alice stepped into the pod and quietly closed the door behind them. It was pitch black inside.

'Lights!' Alice commanded, and the C-Bean was instantly flooded bright white. She was not used to such brightness after being imprisoned in the gloomy cleit, and she was slowly adjusting to it when she heard a quiet but firm voice say, a little sarcastically, 'So you made it. Well done, both of you! Stand with your hands on your heads!'

Alice turned and was shocked to see Karla scowling at her and brandishing a silver penknife. She was even more disturbed when she realised it must be Dr Foster's penknife because it had that yellow shoelace tied to it.

'Right, Donald, you get out now,' Karla's determined voice instructed.

Donald didn't move a muscle, he just kept his eye on the blade glinting in the bright light. All three of them stood absolutely still for what seemed like ages, and then suddenly Karla lunged towards Donald.

'Karla, no!' Alice shrieked as Donald stumbled backwards and fell against the door.

'I'fe been waiting for you, Alice,' she said between gritted teeth. 'This wretched thing will not go anywhere without you. I'fe tried everything.' Karla waved the knife around the interior and stared accusingly at Alice.

Donald saw his chance and moved quickly, grabbing Karla's wrist from behind and twisting her arm, and managed to bring the knife sharply downwards. As he did so, the knife grazed his arm and it started bleeding profusely. Karla's face was now wild with anger and she started wriggling like an animal to free herself from Donald's grip. Donald pulled Karla's arm behind and up her back, but he was shaking again and looked quite frightened.

Alice felt confused and upset to see Karla behaving so strangely, but she knew she needed to do something. She blurted out 'Handcuffs!' and the C-Bean produced a pair. She grabbed them from the recess and Donald managed to wrestle them onto Karla's wrists and remove the knife and the shoulder bag she'd been holding. Karla then seemed to go limp. Donald let go of her. At first she looked as if she was about to drop to the floor with exhaustion, but then suddenly and without warning she crashed out of the door and ran up the hillside. They could hear the familiar sound of her being sick in the grass again. Donald shut the door and leaned against it, panting and still holding her bag.

'That was scary! Are you sure she is who she says she is?'

'You're telling me it was scary. She's been acting so weird the last couple of days. Is your arm all right?' Alice asked in a breathless voice. She pulled a tissue out of her pocket and dabbed the wound.

'Never mind that. Time to go! I'll deal with her. She won't get far now she's got handcuffs on.'

'Neither will I, Donald, unless we get the cardkey back from her and put it in the slot!'

'Maybe it's in her bag,' Donald said, fumbling through its contents. 'Is this it?'

'Yes! It goes in the slot inside the access panel, OK?'

Donald nodded.

Alice tried to calm herself. Her stomach was still tied in knots even though their ordeal appeared to be over, until she realised there was something else nagging at her deep inside. All the time they'd been imprisoned in Lady Grange's cleit, Alice had wanted to escape back to her own time, but right now she found that she was sad to be going. She wanted to give Donald something, some sort of memento. There was nothing in the C-Bean except the knife, which carried all the wrong kind of significance. She felt inside her jeans pockets. Yes, it was still there.

'Close your eyes and hold out your hand.' She gave him the elm tree seedpod.

Donald looked at his palm and smiled.

'I have something to give you, too.'

He took Karla's camera out of his pocket and gave it to her.

'I stole it from the cupboard at the wireless station. I wanted to give you her other machine too, but it wasn't there. You may as well keep this too,' he said, handing her Karla's bag.

They stood silently. Then Donald whispered, 'Can I come with you?'

Alice shook her head and looked down at her wellington boots.

'It's not a good idea, Donald – it could mess everything up. It might have worked in The Time Machine, but we don't know what would happen if someone really did go forwards in time …'

Silence. She took hold of his hand.

'But I will come back, I promise.'

Donald cleared his throat. 'When?'

Alice thought for a moment. Then she had an idea.

'I'll come back on 29th August 1930.'

'Why then?'

'You'll find out, but I can't say.'

'But that's ages, Alice!' Donald rolled his eyes. 'I'll be a grown-up!'

'Let's just hope I recognise you, then, and that you remember who I am!' she joked.

Alice watched as Donald stepped out of the C-Bean, clutching the elm seed and smiling at her.

'I'll put the cardkey in now, all right?' Alice nodded and he closed the door.

'Right, I hope this works – St Kilda, Scotland, 17/05/2018,' she whispered.

✠ ✠ ✠

Instead of the usual routine, the C-Bean did something Alice hadn't seen before. Its walls shimmered through a whole sequence of invalid commands and numbers, like someone was interfering with its memory banks. Next there was a series of images of a place she didn't recognise – the interior of a laboratory building with long grey curving corridors. One image showed the C-Bean itself under construction, standing in a brightly-lit factory space, surrounded by people in green gowns and masks who looked like they were performing a surgical operation.

Then the walls went white and the C-Bean played various audio snippets it must have recorded of Karla's voice getting more and more desperate as she uselessly barked out orders to try and make it depart for 2018. At one point Karla sounded confused, because she said something like 'OK, Plan B then: 16/05/2118.' Another voice replied sharply to Karla's request:

'Negative. Unauthorised command.'

There was a long pause, during which Alice could hear someone moving around, the door of the C-Bean opening and shutting again, and then she heard Karla's voice say, 'Removing cardkey. Activating remote override.'

The walls went black at that point, and a single line of code came up on one wall at eye level. The only actual words Alice could recognise among the string of numbers and letters were 'Operation SeaWAR'.

Alice had no idea what was going on. She stood tense and still in the middle of the space with her arms folded, and waited. More strange images started appearing on the C-Bean's walls, of a missile being fired from a base somewhere and then arcing over a huge expanse of ocean dotted with small rocky islands. She saw images of a rock that looked like one of the stacks near St Kilda exploding, shown as a set of time-lapse photographs of a huge cloud forming in the sky above, billowing upwards and outwards in the shape of a mushroom. On another wall, the C-Bean was running through a huge quantity of other data – graphs, maps and mathematical formulae, like a scientific report – but Alice had no idea what any of it meant.

'I don't understand,' she said aloud, shaking her head.

With that, the C-Bean promptly stopped its technical
show-and-tell, and produced a recess containing a
large sheaf of paperwork in a brown folder tied
up with string. Alice lifted it out of the recess.
On the front cover was a red stamp stating
'Top Secret' printed over black type that
said 'On Her Majesty's Service' and
'Nuclear Weapons Research Programme
– Annual Report 1960'. At that moment, the
door opened. She stuffed the folder along with
the camera into Karla's shoulder bag and stepped warily
out of the C-Bean, already sure she was not in 2018.

☩ ☩ ☩

The C-Bean had arrived way off track this time, and was standing next to
the radar station on the top of Mullach Mor, the second-highest point on
the island. There was a strong wind blowing. The pod had taken its disguise
capabilities to a new level too, appearing this time like a small electrical
substation or generator unit, painted on the outside in a dull military grey,
with a large yellow and black label on the door that said 'DANGER: HIGH
VOLTAGE'. Alice patted it approvingly, and looked around her.

Through the patchy mist, she could see the road going back down the
mountain and could make out the village as a crescent of tiny roofs some way
below her. On closer inspection, a few of the roofs had fallen in and there were
thirty or so khaki green tents erected on the grass between Main Street and
the beach. Alice also noticed that the concrete road leading up to the radar
station actually stopped halfway up the hill, and the rest was just a dirt track as
before, with tools lying around and sacks of cement piled up indicating that

the road was currently under construction. What puzzled her even more than anything was the fact that out to sea there appeared to have been a fire on board a ship, because the bay was filled with a massive cloud of smoke. It had a very distinctive shape, like a tree or a mushroom, exactly like the images she'd just been seeing inside the C-Bean.

Alice was about to head off down the track to investigate further when she caught sight of somebody speaking into a handset inside the radar station. He had a beard and rather untidy hair and was wearing a rough woollen sweater. Alice thought he looked about Karla's age, late twenties maybe, with earnest brown eyes and a deeply furrowed brow. Alice ducked down below the window ledge and crept closer to listen.

'Come in, Benbecula. Yes, sir, picking up some unusual activity in the last hour. Blast zone larger than usual. Seems to have hit Stac Levenish, from what I can make out, plume considerably larger than anything I've seen, now dispersing. Have to say, sir, it looks not unlike what the Yanks dropped on Hiroshima in 1945. I'll put it all in my log, and I've taken photos for the record, but I just thought you should know. Right. No problem. Over and out.' There was a click as the man replaced the handset, a scrape of boots across the wooden floor, and suddenly the door was flung open.

He surveyed her quickly, then a rapid grin flashed across his face.

'I've been expecting you!' he said. 'Robertson, right?'

Alice stood up from her crouched position.

'Alice Robertson, yes. Who are you?'

'James Ferguson. Dad told me about you.'

'Your dad?'

'Yes, my dad, Donald Ferguson.'

They both stared intently at each other and for a fleeting moment Alice thought she could see some similarity between this James and her friend Donald, just as James's gaze shifted from her face to the grey cube behind her. He raised his eyebrows and made a clicking sound with his teeth, then strode over to the C-Bean and knocked against its walls with his knuckles.

'This it, then? Pretty good camouflage.'

'I suppose …' Alice began.

'Well, we have some catching up to do. Have you brought the papers?' he was looking at the bulging shoulder bag.

'I have been given some papers, yes, as it happens,' said Alice slowly, wondering how he could possibly know she would be bringing them, or that she would be arriving at all. It certainly had not been part of her plan.

'It's not safe to talk up here, let's go back to my place, get some lunch. Lie low for a bit.'

And with that James collected his things, locked up the radar station, slipped the keys into his pocket, and strode off down the steepest part of the mountainside. Alice trotted behind him, trying to keep up as they moved through the long wet grass. The smoke cloud in the bay filled the eastern sky and was drifting towards St Kilda.

James lit a small stove, and put the kettle on to boil. He unwrapped some bread and cheese from a tea towel in his little kitchen, and put a jar of pickled beetroot on the table beside it.

'Help yourself,' he said, while he washed two mugs and swilled out a yellow teapot.

'Is this the same house as your dad lived in?' asked Alice, looking around the simply furnished room with its bed, armchair, table and stove, and remembering her friend darting into a house the day of the submarine attack.

'Certainly is. When I was first stationed here earlier this year, they wanted to put me in the old wireless station, which was done up as proper living accommodation, but once I'd worked out which house had belonged to my family, I repaired the roof and moved in here. It was the first one to get done up.'

'Do you work here all year round?'

'Yes. The War Office has been granted the right to have a missile tracking station here, but the National Trust for Scotland are in charge of the island. I'm the operator in charge of monitoring things up at the new radar station.'

Alice had so many questions bubbling up inside her, but something in James's manner assured her they would have time to work it all out. For now, she just needed to check one thing.

'James. What year is it?'

'1957.'

'OK. And was the island evacuated in 1930?'

'Yes, all thirty-six of us that were left, when I was a baby. I was the last one to be born on St Kilda. That's my claim to fame!' He laughed and clapped his palms against his thighs, making the table wobble. Hot tea slopped onto the breadboard.

'And your dad?'

James looked down at his feet and paused for a moment before he answered her.

'He's dead, sorry to tell you. Got himself involved in active service in the Second World War as a pilot, survived pretty much the whole war and was then brought down during some mission in July 1944. The whole crew perished and they never found the bodies. He was a pretty brave guy, though, got awarded the Victoria Cross – funnily enough for taking out a German submarine when he was stationed in Italy. I have it here.'

James pulled open a drawer in a carved wooden chest beside his bed, and took out a navy blue box. Inside on a bed of dark red velvet lay Donald's medal. Alice lifted it out, remembering his boyish blood-stained face in the midst of his first experience of war – just an hour before in terms of her time.

'He talked about you a lot, Alice. Told us all kinds of fantastical bedtime stories when we were growing up, about this girl who could travel through time, and what she got up to in her time-travel machine.'

Alice smiled. 'I'm sure most of it was made up.'

'Well, I know one part was true. Did you not notice something in the backyard?'

James took her outside and round to the rear of the tiny dwelling. There, growing among the tussocks of grass, was a small but determined-looking elm tree, its slender branches twisting and swaying in the fierce St Kildan breeze. Alice chuckled and did a quick calculation in her head. There was no doubt in her mind it was the elm seed that Donald must have planted back in 1918 after she left, which meant it was now thirty-nine years old.

'So after you left Dad in 1918, after that German sub attacked, what happened next?' James asked conspiratorially once they were back inside his cottage.

'I don't know, because it hasn't happened yet.'

'What do you mean?'

'Well, I was trying to get back to 2018 just now, and I ended up here. From what I can make out, the C-Bean will only travel back in time to the same date and time but in a different year.'

Alice looked at her watch, 'Let me check to make sure: I make it 12 noon on 17th May, right?'

James consulted his watch. 'Correct.'

'Something weird happened in the C-Bean when I was trying to issue the command, and I've ended up here.'

'To be honest, I wasn't surprised you showed up today – first there was a weird explosion out in the bay, then just as you arrived I was picking up something else odd too, a radio signal up at the station. On a frequency no one's ever used before.'

Alice remembered the folder and pulled it out of Karla's bag.

'You asked to see this,' she reminded James, and pushed the bread and cheese aside to make room for it on the table.

James's eyes grew wide as they fell on the stamp on the front cover. Without a word, he tugged at the string holding it all together, and took a deep breath before opening it.

'1960... crikey, that's three years into the future. Where did you get this?' he breathed.

'The C-Bean... obtained it,' Alice said in a hushed voice.

James was rifling through the pages, as if he was looking for something he knew would be in there. There were detailed maps of Scotland in one section – Alice recognised the familiar outlines – with red dots marked all around the coast. There were other maps of clusters of islands elsewhere, on pages entitled 'Nuclear Test Sites'.

'I knew it,' James suddenly declared triumphantly, stabbing his forefinger at a map Alice could see was of St Kilda. 'The idiots!'

'What is it? What have you found?'

'That wasn't just a routine missile they launched from Benbecula earlier. It was a nuclear warhead!'

Alice glanced at the page he was studying and her stomach turned when saw printed in block capitals the words 'Operation SeaWAR'. As if reading her thoughts, James continued, 'Bet that's why you've been thrown off course – I knew about them detonating bombs in the Australian outback and off Christmas Island in the South Pacific, but I had no idea about plans to test them here in Britain! Didn't we learn anything from Hiroshima back in 1945?' He growled under his breath and shook his head.

'They said the death of more than a hundred thousand people was the price we had to pay to end the war and that it would never happen again, but look, this is the report of us Brits carrying out a test explosion of a nuclear bomb right here off St Kilda!'

Alice looked at the photographs dated 17th May 1957 and realised they were the same time-lapse images that the C-Bean had been displaying just before she arrived. It must have been happening in real time.

'And what's more, I was right – they are storing weapons-grade nuclear material somewhere on St Kilda, as well as planning to dump spent nuclear fuel rods and warheads here. It says this is the first British site to be selected,' James said angrily.

He was running his finger impatiently down page after page.

'Doesn't say exactly where they are dumping stuff, but I'm sure I'll find it. I've been picking up unidentified ships from the radar station arriving from the north side of the island and delivering something I thought was suspicious, so I've been logging their movements – but so far no one has acknowledged what's actually going on.'

James sat back and tugged his beard, his face going through a sequence of pained expressions, finally settling on that deeply furrowed brow Alice had seen earlier.

'OK, we've got our work cut out. We'll take a boat trip round the perimeter of the island and check it out thoroughly. I don't know why I haven't done it already.'

'But I need to get home,' Alice said, 'I'm not sure I should stay that long.'

James looked at her and scratched his head.

'I promise we'll be back by teatime and you'll be on your way, but there's no point you going back unless we know for sure.'

'Know what? And who are 'they' exactly? You keep saying 'they'.' Alice was feeling a bit cross – what James was saying just didn't make sense to her.

'You've arrived in the middle of what everyone's calling the Cold War, Alice. It's not a war that's being fought in the open, like a real battle as such. Countries like America and Russia are spying on each other. They're accusing one another of lying about how many and what kind of weapons they each have, and all the while they're both busy secretly designing and building a deadly nuclear arsenal! Now, as if it couldn't get any worse, it seems Britain is building up a deadly stockpile of its own. They've been calling me a conspiracy theorist for years Alice, but now I almost have proof. However, your Top Secret file isn't going to be enough – we need to get some actual hard evidence. I'm absolutely positive we are either making, storing or testing nuclear weapons right here on St Kilda, Alice. Probably all three. And it's got to be stopped!'

James made various growling noises again and started making preparations for their expedition, his movements quick and deft. He filled a metal canister with water and proceeded to pack a small rucksack with binoculars, a compass, two gas masks and a boxy-looking camera in a brown leather case. He looked in the chest by his bed, took out three rolls of photographic film and stuffed them in a side pocket. In the other side pocket he put a box of matches.

'Got what you need?' he asked Alice, who was already a little absent-minded at the prospect of this expedition.

Alice looked in Karla's shoulder bag. There was a packet of tissues, a granola bar and her camera.

'This could be useful,' she said, switching on the camera. 'In fact …' she scrolled through the last few photographs, and it felt strange seeing images of St Kilda that had in reality taken place thirty-nine years ago, but from Alice's point of view they'd only just been taken in the past hour.

'James, look – I have some pictures of your dad here.'

'Really?'

James put the rucksack down and took the camera gingerly in his hands, as if it were an injured bird.

'What do I press?'

'Here, like this.'

Alice watched as he scanned her scenes of war-torn St Kilda, with his own father, a twelve-year-old boy, caught in the thick of it. James sniffed and a tear rolled down one cheek. Alice offered him one of Karla's tissues from the bag. The last picture was of Dora's face appearing in the doorway of the C-Bean, her features wracked with worry. James blew his nose loudly and suddenly grinned.

'That's Granny Dora, if I'm not mistaken! She looks so young – incredible.'

He was distracted for a moment by the force of his own memories. Then he shook his head, stroking his beard.

'Right, this is no time for nostalgia. Let's go.'

Outside, the wind had dropped. James took a direct route once again, striking a line towards the jetty, with Alice struggling to keep up. She still had no clear idea of what they were going to look for, or what James was so keen to find out.

James stopped to load film into his camera, and then started taking photographs of the plume, which Alice could see was drifting slowly towards the neighbouring island of Boreray.

'Who's on St Kilda at the moment, James? What are all those tents doing in the Village?'

'That's RAF and army people who are here to construct the facilities. Luckily for you, they're not around today, thank goodness – went off on some recce.'

'Recce?'

'You know – a reconnaissance mission – to Boreray. Oh and a couple of high-up War Office guys are supposed to be arriving later today to check on progress if the weather holds; and in a month or so some nature conservation guys will descend on the island for the summer. They're planning to come every year from now on, to mend walls and log bird colonies and such. Mind you, by the time they get here I wouldn't be surprised if the whole place is radioactive.'

'What does "radioactive" mean, exactly?'

'Well, for starters, it means you should be wearing one of these.' James pulled the two gas masks out of his rucksack and slid one down over his face.

He pulled it away from his mouth to add, 'It's dangerous stuff. Makes people really ill in all sorts of ways. Some scientists even think it even causes cancer. That device they detonated today is only a fraction of the size the Americans dropped on Hiroshima and Nagasaki in Japan, but it looks like it's wiped out a massive bird population in the first few seconds. Officially, I'm keeping an eye on things, but unofficially, I'm keeping notes on all this top secret activity, in order to get the evidence to support my theories.'

'Theories?' Alice asked, struggling with her mask.

'Britain is getting involved in the nuclear arms race, and it's only a matter of time before it all goes horribly wrong. The Americans and Russians are way ahead of us in terms of developing technologies of mass destruction. If we are all at it, there'll soon be enough nuclear weapons to destroy the entire planet, and even if only a couple of them went off it could kill half the world's population straight off, pollute our seas and farmland with radiation for the next hundred years and leave the survivors suffering the consequences of radiation sickness for the rest of their lives. I want to do something to stop it right now, before it's too late. That test explosion you saw today is just the start – there'll be much worse to come.'

'And you think there's a secret stash of radioactive nuclear stuff right here on the island?'

'That's one of my theories, yep. And if the past few weeks are anything to go by, a new shipment is due today. If we hurry we might just catch them red-handed delivering it. Now, keep your mask on, Alice.'

They were jogging past all the military tents down to the shore where there was a small wooden dinghy with an outboard motor moored against the jetty. James slung his rucksack into the bottom of the boat and started untying the rope. Alice noticed the name SEABEAN was painted in green capitals on the back of the boat.

'I like what you called it,' she said through the mask, but James didn't hear her. He just pointed for her to step aboard and put on a lifejacket.

Alice zipped up her fleece and then pulled the lifejacket on and settled herself on the wooden seat in the middle of the boat. There were oars in the bottom, but James started up the engine and they pulled away.

'We'll take some more photos of the explosion on Levenish and then go round to the north side and take a look from there – that's where this new radio signal seemed to be coming from!' James shouted through his mask over the roar of the engine and the slop of the waves. Alice just nodded and pressed her knees together to try to avoid shivering. They skirted alongside the neighbouring island of Dùn, moving towards its southernmost tip. The grey sea was choppy and waves were coming over the bows of the boat. Alice realised she had never been round St Kilda in a boat before and it was much bigger than she'd previously thought. The cliffs soared above them, a seething mass of wildlife. She felt a little nauseous with the lurching motion of the boat and the smell of petrol, and was worried she might be sick in the mask.

James then took them several hundred metres out into the middle of Village Bay and stood in the middle of the boat to take more photographs of the devastated sea stack with his camera. The boat was moving around a lot in the waves and Alice gripped onto the rail, hoping James would not take too long. Gannets and fulmars were diving and squealing all around them, still in a state of alarm. Floating all around the boat were the remains of hundreds of dead birds, their feathers burned and charred. James shook his head with disapproval at the devastation, and then they moved east towards the cliffs opposite, below the mountain of Oiseval – the same route the German submarine had taken in 1918.

As James took the tiller again and steered the dinghy round the headland, Alice thought she could hear another boat's engine in the distance, but couldn't be sure – the wind and the birds were making so much noise. Ahead of them Alice could see two large brown birds attacking a group of fulmars by diving towards them at speed and tipping their wings so they lost balance and dropped into the sea. The fulmars in a panic dropped their gulletfuls of fish and the brown birds seized the fish for themselves, amid much squawking and commotion.

Alice pointed to the scavengers and shouted, 'Look out James! Bonxies!'

'What are they?' James shouted, watching the birds in astonishment.

'Haven't you seen them before? Their proper name is Arctic skua – our teacher Dr Foster told us they are the real villains of the seas. They don't bother catching their own fish, just steal everyone else's.'

'No, never seen anything like that before,' James called, watching their antics intently.

From behind them, there was a sudden roar, and when Alice turned towards the sound, a much larger boat painted a dark military grey had emerged from behind a stack of rock and was coming straight at them.

'James, look out!' Alice shouted as the boat sped past, sending up spray and making their dinghy rock violently from side to side. Alice read the name on the stern – *Dark Hunter*. At that moment James turned, lost his footing and fell overboard, his camera still around his neck. Someone on the other boat was shouting something through a loudhailer, but Alice couldn't hear properly. Meanwhile James had disappeared under the water. Alice checked on all sides of the boat but there was no sign of him. *Seabean's* engine was still idling. Her heart thumping in her chest, Alice moved to the back of the boat and sat down next to the tiller, trying to remember which way to push it to steer a boat left or right. The other boat was turning up ahead, about to come back in their direction. Alice managed to turn *Seabean* to face the cliffs, and then spotted James waving about ten metres away. She edged nearer and he clambered aboard, shivering and dripping wet.

'Go, Alice, just go! That's one of the Navy's new fast patrol boats. Head for those rocks, I know a cave under there where we can hide.'

Alice opened the engine's throttle and the boat surged forward, the bows rising high out of the water. She could hear the other boat behind them, but didn't dare look round.

'Are they following us?' she called to James, who lay in the bottom of the boat in front of her. He didn't answer. Alice pressed on towards the rugged coastline of St Kilda. She could see a darker archway in the lower part of the cliffs, and aimed for that, hoping it was the cave James meant.

'James, are you OK?' she yelled again. Still no response. Something whistled past her head and cracked off the rocks ahead of her. And again. She realised the other boat was firing at theirs. More bullets whined past. Alice ducked down as low as she could. One bullet glanced off the edge of the boat, leaving a deep scorch mark in the varnish. They were nearing the cave entrance, so she had to slow down. Alice risked a quick look over her shoulder. She could see the dark silhouette of a man standing on the deck of the boat behind, operating a gun. She shuddered and turned to face forward – the *Seabean* was entering the mouth of the cave. A seal barked at them from the rocks, then wriggled into the deep water, its echo bouncing off the cave walls. Alice realised they would be safe here, since the entrance to the cave was much too small for the larger boat to pass through. She decided to try and moor *Seabean* alongside the rocks where the seal had been basking and see if James was all right. But there was no mooring, so she just made the engine cut out.

James was still lying face down in the boat. Alice moved forwards, calling his name. He felt cold and didn't seem to be breathing. Alice tried not to panic, and remembered how Edie's mum felt your pulse. With some difficulty she managed to free James's left arm from under him and squeezed the inside of his wrist. She realised to her relief he was alive but unconscious. There was no sign of the camera.

'OK, now what?' Alice muttered to herself. She looked at her watch. It was coming up to three o'clock. She could hear the *Dark Hunter's* engine humming just outside the cave. She could feel her own pulse racing. James groaned suddenly and tried to roll over. The bottom of the boat was full of water. Alice helped him to sit up, opened his rucksack and made him sip some water from the metal canister he'd brought.

'Have they gone?' James asked after he'd taken a few mouthfuls.

'Not yet, no,' Alice whispered, taking a slurp herself and wiping her chin.

Her eyes had got used to the dimness of the cave now, and she stared around her. Higher up on the rocks beside them she could see that some equipment had been stacked. It looked like drums of explosives and coils of rope, and ten or twelve spherical devices painted black.

'Look up there, James – what are they?' Alice asked, dreading his reply.

James rubbed his eyes and stared in the direction Alice was pointing.

'Good God! Naval mines, if I'm not mistaken.'

'What are they for?'

'They are basically bombs that are planted underwater to blow up submarines. We used them in the war to create safe zones for own ships and also to attack enemy U-boats. There are ships called minesweepers that go around making sure the sea is safe from mines for other naval vessels. I've picked up reports that the American navy is planning to use dolphins to detect and lay mines in future.'

'Really? That's not good,' Alice said, frowning. 'Have these ones exploded yet or not?'

'They look intact to me. Goodness knows what they're using them for in the Cold War. Have you got that other camera, Alice? We should take some shots of them.'

Alice took Karla's camera out of her bag and offered it to James.

'You do it – I have no idea how that thing of yours works!'

Alice took a panoramic shot inside the cave, moving the camera in video mode steadily from left to right until she was facing the mouth of the cave.

'I think they've gone,' James remarked. 'We should get going.'

He tried to ease himself up, and winced with pain.

'What's the matter, James? Where is it hurting?'

'My ankle – I must have twisted it as I fell into the water. Can you be captain?'

Alice nodded, and was about to pull the starter rope when James waved his arms for her to stop.

'Use the oars, Alice, until we get outside. I want to be sure they've gone.'

Alice used one oar to push them away from the rocks, then struggled to manoeuvre both oars into position. Facing the back of the boat, she began to pull them through the water in small circles, gaining momentum, while James steered with the tiller.

'More to the left, Alice,' he muttered. 'That's it. Not much further.'

Alice's hands were cold and wet, and the oars kept slipping.

'OK, pull them in now. We'll just drift out.'

As they re-emerged into the daylight, the sound of James's voice changed, no longer echoing off the cave walls. He was peering through his binoculars, scanning the cliffs in both directions.

'We can't go back to Village Bay, Alice. That's where they will have headed. We'll have to go round to the Gleann Mor side and walk back.'

'How are you going to do that with a twisted ankle?' Alice asked.

'We'll just have to.'

✠ ✠ ✠

They landed later that afternoon in Gleann Mor, cold, hungry and exhausted. There was no beach as such, so having wedged the *Seabean's* mooring rope with a knot between two rocks, they gathered their belongings and made a start inland. What with their wet clothes, James's swollen ankle and the fierce southwesterly wind, they made very slow progress up the valley. Alice was instinctively heading for the pass at the top, just below the radar station. But James was in a lot of pain, and she could not imagine how they were going to make it back to his house. Then she had another idea.

'We'll rest in the Amazon's house, James – do you know it?'

'Aye, it's that haunted stone dwelling near here. I've not been inside it. People have said there's something odd about it.'

Alice felt drawn to the place ever since she'd had a strange experience there a few months before, when she thought she had felt the presence of the ancient female warrior. It made her shiver even now, and it wasn't just the cold this time.

She could see the outline of the stone dwelling in the distance. James's limping was getting slower and slower, but eventually they made it. Alice had nothing with which to strap up his ankle, and no blankets to keep him warm. She spread the contents of James's rucksack out to dry on the stone ledges built into the walls. Alice remembered finding an engraved metal tag on a chain on one of the ledges last time. There were a few other ragged bits of metal debris strewn around, but she couldn't see the chain anywhere. James slumped down, unable to walk any further.

The only things that had survived their sea voyage were the canister of water, Karla's camera and a soggy granola bar. Alice split the granola bar in half, and ate her portion as she pondered her next move. As a bare minimum they needed food, dry clothes and something to support James's ankle. She might not manage to get James safely back to his house, but she could leave him here so long as he was comfortable, and if she was lucky she might even make it back home to 2018 before nightfall.

Alice left James sleeping and zig-zagged up the last section of the valley. It was steep and she was tiring quickly after the exertions of the day. As she rested by a pile of rocks halfway up, she thought she could just make out the outline of the C-Bean flickering faintly against the sky. But she must have been so tired she was imagining it, because when she finally reached the ridge, all she found there was the radar station. Telling herself that the C-Bean must have made itself invisible again, she ran around desperately hoping she would somehow bump into it. But however much she searched the area beside the radar station where she'd left it, she could not find the C-Bean's smooth walls anywhere.

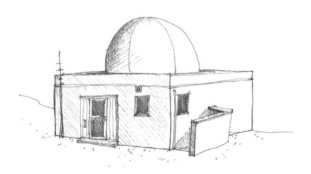

Alice pressed on. As she reached the village, she could hear voices and a boat chugging in the bay. It was difficult to say for sure in the gathering twilight, but she thought she could just see the outline of the *Dark Hunter* that had pursued them earlier. She realised they must have been the War Office men James had mentioned would be arriving. Alice wasted no time, and quietly let herself in to James's house. There was a torch on the shelf by the front door, and she used it to look around for the items they needed. She found crackers, a jar of salmon paste, a bottle of lemonade, dry clothes and a blanket, matches, a couple of candles and some aspirin, but no bandages, so she took a long knitted scarf instead. She stuffed everything into Karla's shoulder bag and then, as an afterthought, went back for James's pillow. There was a brown notebook under the pillow, which she decided to take as well. She thought about making up a flask of hot tea for James, but she didn't know how to operate the stove and anyway it was a lot to carry back up the mountain and over into the valley on the other side.

All set for the return journey to Gleann Mor, Alice crouched outside James's front door and listened intently, scanning the village and the tents for any sign of human activity. One or two tents were lit from inside and there was a light on in what Alice knew as Reverend Sinclair's house. No doubt that was where the War Office men were staying.

She groped her way between the rocks and cleitean that were dotted everywhere in the grass, heading towards the wall that ran along behind the village. She paused for a moment to catch her breath, then climbed over it, and began the climb back up to the ridge. It was almost dark when she reached it and her legs had turned to jelly, so she half ran, half fell down into Gleann Mor, and managed to find the stone house where she'd left James. It was silent inside, and smelled strongly of bird droppings.

'James, are you there?' Alice called, softly in case he was still asleep.

But James wasn't there. She put all the things down, turned on the torch and looked round, inside and out, calling his name into the darkness. Nothing. In the end she was so exhausted, she made a small bed for herself with the pillow and blanket and curled up to sleep.

✠ ✠ ✠

As the sun was breaking over the ridge to the north-east, she could feel its rays boring into her face, and when she opened her eyes she thought she could see the outline of a man in a flying jacket standing in front of her. Alice called out 'Who are you?' but the person drifted away. The light was too strong and made her head throb with pain, so she closed her eyes again. Her throat was dry and she felt sore where her wet clothes had chafed her skin the day before. In a panic, she awoke fully. It was 7 am.

There was still no sign of James, no footprints, nothing. A stream trickled past the stone dwelling. She lay on her stomach beside it and drank some of the cool fresh spring water. She ate some of the crackers, then repacked Karla's shoulder bag including the torch and James's notebook, leaving the rest of his things there. Then she set off to look for him. She headed for the radar station once more, harbouring a small hope that as she rounded the summit she would see that her beloved C-Bean had returned.

No such luck. And worse still, the War Office men were inside the radar station with the door open. She crept up to the back of the building and held her breath.

'Where the dickens do you think Ferguson's gone?' said one in a gruff, angry tone.

'No idea. His last report was filed yesterday morning. He knows things he shouldn't have got wind of, that's for sure. Lord knows what he was up to yesterday, and who that girl was he had with him. They must have gone into hiding somewhere.'

'Well, she is obviously working for him. Hope he doesn't try and pull a stunt like that again. He'll get court-martialled for it.'

'Yes sir, he's finished.'

'He obviously knows about the cave.'

'Knows too much, that's for sure. Probably working for the other side, I shouldn't wonder.'

'Commies! No matter, we'll search his place later, see if there's anything there. Bound to have got some dodgy evidence together by now.'

Alice let out a little involuntary gasp when she heard this and remembered she'd left the top secret file in the house. She didn't want James to get into any more trouble, so she realised to her dismay she needed to go back and fetch it. Alice darted round to the front of the radar station and surveyed the hillside in front of her. There was no cover, and the only thing she could do was run as fast as she could down the hillside, hoping they would not see her. But they were on their guard and within seconds she heard one of them shout 'You, girl, wait!'

But Alice didn't look back, she just kept running. The footsteps behind were gaining on her rapidly. Out of breath, she turned and saw both men had guns and were moving expertly through the grass. Ahead of her were some stone cleitean. Alice ducked inside the biggest one, hoping they would not see where she had disappeared. Fighting back angry tears, she crawled to the darkest corner and waited.

✠ ✠ ✠

Alice's heart was still racing, but she was fairly sure the men couldn't have seen her duck inside the cleit or they would have found her by now. She held her breath and listened hard for several more minutes with her eyes shut. When she finally opened them, all she could make out were a few chinks of daylight coming through gaps in the stone walls, along with the wind. Her eyes slowly adjusted to the gloom inside the cleit. There was something quite familiar about its size and height. She vaguely thought she could hear Karla sniffing in the darkness, but decided her mind must be playing tricks on her – it just felt like the cleit where they'd been imprisoned in 1918. The sniffing got louder, and someone cleared their throat.

'I don't suppose you've brought me paper and a pen as I requested.' It was not Karla's German accent, but a crisp, faintly Scottish female voice.

There was a rustle of fabric and a tall, gaunt woman appeared a few feet from where Alice was crouching. The woman wore a long dress with a very full dark blue skirt and a cream lace neckline. She had pale, papery skin, green eyes and red curly hair piled up on top of her head with hairpins, and wore a choker of pearls around her throat. On closer inspection, Alice noticed the woman's boots were dirty and worn, and the hem of the dress was caked in mud. She seemed confused when she saw Alice.

'Oh! Who, pray, are you child? Why are you here? – my breakfast tray has already been returned.'

'My name is Alice. I am trying to escape from those men.'

'As am I,' the woman said wearily, and smoothed a hand over her skirt. 'I have been detained here against my will for years and years. No one has come for me. It's a national disgrace.' Her voice grew quickly shrill and angry, and her eyes took on a fiery look.

Alice bit her lip, and then in a very quiet voice asked, 'You wouldn't by any chance be Lady Grange, would you?'

'I am she, yes, it is true,' the woman said airily, with what was left of her noble manner, and then added with a tut, 'Never was there ever such an unladylike place as this!'

'So it's true …' Alice murmured to herself. She couldn't remember how long ago this lady had been imprisoned on St Kilda, but it was several centuries for sure. How had she slipped so far back in time? Alice was deeply puzzled, but also aware that this new turn of events had in any case saved her from being captured by the War Office men in 1957. Had she somehow accidentally stepped inside the C-Bean without realising or remembering? After she bumped her head badly back in April, they said at Glasgow General Hospital she might suffer occasional lapses of short-term memory. Had something just happened up on the mountainside that she was unable to recall?

Lady Grange was pacing up and down, muttering to herself as if she too was searching for some lost memory. Alice stood up and looked around the cleit. In one corner there was a straw mattress, similar to the one she had slept on when she was imprisoned, and a foul-smelling bucket. Right beside it was an elegant little chair and an antique writing desk, on which stood a small vase containing a tall, straggly wild flower.

Lady Grange watched as Alice approached the table. It seemed so out of place in this rough interior.

'What is the use of a writing table if they never let me write?' Lady Grange scoffed, and flung herself down on the mattress. After a while she asked in a softer, more curious tone, 'Pray tell me, how is it you speak English? Why have they dressed you in such strange attire? And what is in your bag, child?'

In all the palaver, Alice had forgotten she still had Karla's shoulder bag with her.

'Actually, I have some food. Are you hungry, Lady Grange?' Alice asked politely, as she pulled out the bottle of lemonade, the rest of the crackers and the jar of salmon paste.

'No, I have no need of sustenance now. My stomach it too disturbed today.' There was a long pause, and then she said, 'You can call me Rachel if you like, since you're a fellow prisoner. I am guessing it is the first time you have been held against your will.'

'The second time, actually,' Alice admitted, opening the bottle of lemonade slowly and listening to the long hiss as the bubbles escaped.

'I also have paper and a pencil, if you're interested.'

Lady Grange sat up instantly, her eyes alert and blinking. It was too dark to see properly inside the cleit, but sensing the woman's urgent need to write, Alice laid James's brown notebook on the writing desk and opened it at an empty page. Lady Grange fairly snatched the pencil from her hand, and then seated herself very carefully at the desk.

'Oh for a candle!' she wailed despairingly.

Alice searched the cleit and found an ornate brass candlestick on the ground, but no candle. Then she remembered James's torch.

'Just a moment, I have something better.'

Lady Grange was startled by the sudden brilliance of the torch's beam. She looked at Alice with fresh eyes, and her tone became more humble.

'Who *are* you, my dear? Do you come from foreign shores?'

'No, I live here, like you. Just in another time.'

Lady Grange frowned. 'What time are you speaking of?'

Alice looked at her watch and her stomach turned a somersault as she remembered how long she had now been missing.

'Friday 18th May 2018, 8.30 am, to be exact. I should be arriving in the schoolyard on St Kilda right now.'

When she heard this, Lady Grange stood up abruptly from the desk and backed away from Alice, and James's torch and notebook fell to the ground. Alice stepped forward to pick them up, as the room seemed to spin slightly, and she felt strangely dizzy all of a sudden. The last thing she heard was Lady Grange's shrill voice saying, 'What is happening? This must stop at once!'

Alice's Blog #3

Saturday 19th May 2018

It's such a relief to be home! Either the C-Bean came back to fetch me or it had been standing there on the hillside all along — disguising itself so well as a stone cleit that it even had me fooled. When I crawled inside it to get away from those men in 1957 I had no idea! Charlie found me all disorientated, lying on the floor of the C-Bean clutching James's torch and notebook. He said he thought he saw Karla dressed in a funny costume run out of the C-Bean the moment it appeared back in the schoolyard, but it was actually Lady Grange. Nobody knew anything about her existence until late yesterday afternoon when Mrs Butterfield found her sleeping in the store behind the shop. She'd stolen a whole pad of paper and a set of gel pens and had been feverishly drawing and writing, apparently.

She's been given Karla's old room above the pub now, and Karla's wardrobe of black clothes. She thought they were boys' clothes at first, but in the end she seemed glad to change out of her tatty old dress. She keeps talking about needing to get back to Edinburgh, only she hasn't got any money to pay for the ferry crossing. So Mrs Butterfield says she can stay and work in the shop until she's got enough together to cover the journey. But she keeps wandering off, and people say they saw her wandering all over the island yesterday. It's like she was imprisoned in that cleit for so long that she just needs to roam freely now. Edie's mum rang the doctor on the mainland and he's sending over some special medicine to help calm her down. No one has any idea how she got here, or why she arrived dressed in a sort of theatrical costume.

All in all I'd been gone for three whole days. As far as my parents were concerned, Karla and I were stuck inside the C-Bean without food and water and they couldn't get it to open. Charlie assured them that the C-Bean could provide us with things to eat and drink via its vending function, and that it probably had its own oxygen supply too, but they were still freaking out – mainly because of my recent head injury. Anyway, they were more bothered about me than about Karla. They think Karla has gone AWOL – that's 'absent without leave' - and they've put out a Missing Person announcement on Scottish radio and on the Internet. I couldn't understand at first why everyone seemed so suspicious about Karla, until Charlie told me that while I was gone, he found her passport with a completely different name on it in her office. It turns out she doesn't work for a company making high-tech learning pods for the education market like she said, and when Charlie's dad made some enquiries, the police on the mainland looked into it and said she had a criminal record as a computer hacker. So she is a spy after all! Charlie thinks it's really hilarious that Karla's now a prisoner of war in the twentieth century and instead I've come back with another prisoner that I've accidentally freed from the eighteenth century.

I suppose it's pretty cool that I've rescued Lady Grange, because it was really unfair what her husband did to her, but I still feel bad about what happened to Karla. Then yesterday Charlie and I managed to get the files off her camera onto our computer and we now reckon she's been spying on us the whole time - by the looks of things she's not really the C-Bean's designer at all, and came here under a false name to nick the idea and email loads of information about it back to Germany so they could try and make one of their own. When we showed my parents Karla's photos, Dad gave us a passionate lecture about 'industrial espionage' and 'reverse engineering' – he's always been worried about that kind of thing – like whether someone would steal his ideas for the wave energy machines before they were built. Poor Dad - the whole thing with me disappearing has made him more stressed and sick than ever – he gets headaches all the time now, and his skin is even more red and itchy. I feel really bad about it, and what's more Charlie said his dad is feeling worse too.

On the plus side, Charlie and I have checked up on a few things that went right about my time travel adventure. For instance, I was so happy when we looked up the births and deaths in the chapel's ledgers and saw that the newborn babies stopped dying after 1851, and there is even a note dated 16th May 1851 saying they prayed and gave thanks for the mysterious hamper of food and medicines!

Sunday 20th May 2018

I've been worrying a lot about what happened to James after I left him in the Amazon's house, and whether he is OK. What if the War Office men found the file I gave him? So we've been trying to find out what happened to James and to Donald. This morning Charlie and I looked up on the Internet what 'court-martialled' means, and apparently it's some kind of law court for when soldiers have done something wrong. Charlie thinks that when they said he must be 'working for the other side' they meant the Russians, and that James was therefore some kind of spy too, but I don't think he was. He just didn't want Britain to carry on making all those nasty bombs and ruining St Kilda in the process.

When we went to church this morning, it was really weird seeing Donald Ferguson's name listed on the Second World War plaque in the chapel as one of the St Kildan men to have perished in 1944, just like James told me. What's more, we also found Donald's dad's grave in the graveyard. James, however, is a bit more of a mystery. Apart from what we already know, that is: he really was the last baby to be born on St Kilda, on 3rd August 1930, and his mother was called Elsa Gillies. The rest is a bit hazy. His name appears on a list of all the people working on the island in 1957, but it doesn't say what happened to him after that. So I don't know if he was caught and punished, or escaped, or what! There were a few other things on the Internet but we have no idea if any of it relates to James. For example, there was a James Ferguson nominated for a Nobel Peace Prize in 1977, but it doesn't seem likely it was the same person, and another James Ferguson who filed a patent for a synthetic black material called Obsidon in the UK in 2002. We also found a news report from the same year which said the production plant in China that won the contract to manufacture Obsidon had burned down.

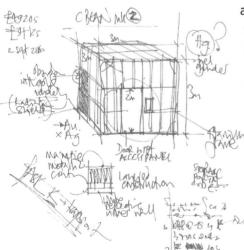

The only other clues about James are in his notebook, which Charlie and I have gone through really thoroughly, but there is not much we could understand. He was obviously keeping a kind of diary about the government's plans to make and store nuclear weapons in Scotland, like he told me. There is even a drawing of the same mushroom cloud after the explosion on 17th May, and underneath he's written something about it all leading to ruin. Weirdly, there are some entries dated 1960, where he's written down a load of ideas and maths calculations about time travel, including a diagram of the C-Bean, no doubt based on what Donald told him. He was obviously getting muddled up about dates, what with all his fantasising about travelling to the future, because he's even written underneath one diagram 'Activation date: November 2017'. He got one thing wrong from Donald, though: it's titled 'C-Bean Mark 2'

Tuesday 29th May 2018

The C-Bean Mark 3 has disappeared! It was there in the schoolyard when we came home from school yesterday afternoon. Mum had been doing a history lesson about the Second World War in the C-Bean with us, and it showed us black and white films with Japanese survivors telling their stories about the awful things that happened to their families and their cities after they dropped the atom bombs. Charlie and I were asking her why people still wanted to make nuclear weapons when they knew how horrible the effects could be, and then the C-Bean did this strange thing it had never done before — an alert message flashed up on all the walls saying, 'File missing. Could not retrieve data.' Afterwards I wondered if it was because I'd given that particular file to James.

The thing I'm most upset about now the C-Bean has disappeared is that Charlie and I were planning to go back to 1957 and check to see if James is OK. I'm still hoping that the C-Bean has just gone invisible for some reason and we will run into it soon. But I've got a nasty feeling this might all be Karla's doing.

The C-Bean had been missing for several weeks. Alice and Charlie had almost got out of their daily habit of arriving early for school so that they could search the schoolyard, looking for any kind of clue as to its whereabouts. One weekend, Alice had traced over a map of the whole village and they'd divided it into a hundred squares to search the bay more systematically. All six children had checked their bit of the map thoroughly. The only things they'd found were a toggle that must have fallen off Dr Foster's duffle coat, a few old coins, a shell from a bullet, which they decided must have been one the German submarine fired, and, in the back of Sam F's garden, the stump of a tree, which Alice realised was where Donald had planted the elm tree in the Fergusons' back garden.

Old Jim came out to see what they were doing on the first day. He stood in front of his underground house for ages, nodding his approval, and coughing violently from time to time. Spex ran backwards and forwards between them, barking excitedly. The second day, Jim only came out for a little while, and stood there shivering even though it was quite a warm day. In the end, Alice and Edie were worried about him, and helped him back inside to bed.

Alice began using James's notebook to write down her own theories and observations. On one page she drew a picture of the half-grown elm tree as she remembered it. Opposite she drew their new tree, the Scots pine, and wrote underneath it, 'Actually the SECOND tree to have been planted on the island'. On another page she made a detailed drawing of the C-Bean Mark 3, with all its special features and capabilities labelled and listed so she wouldn't forget them. She also printed out some of the pictures from 1918 that she'd managed to get off Karla's camera and stuck those in, but she didn't date them. The notebook became a source of comfort, she took to sleeping with it under her pillow like James had done, and after a while she started carrying it everywhere she went, so that she had images of the C-Bean with her even if she didn't have the real thing anymore.

On the last day of the summer term, their teacher Mrs Robertson asked the children to write and draw pictures of the best memories from their past school year. For Alice, this was finally too much, and she fled out of the classroom in tears, unable to even begin to put down on paper what had started to seem a crazy dream that never really happened. She ran as far from the school as she could get, and ended up near Old Jim's underground house. She plunged her hands into her pockets and stood with the fresh summer wind whipping her face and hair, staring out to sea. Her fingers curled around the edges of the notebook in her left pocket. In between the gusts of wind she caught the sound of Jim's coughing. Alice turned and called out his name. Spex crept out of the house and greeted her, quietly wagging his tail.

'Hey Spex, is Jim still poorly?'

Alice ruffled the fur round his neck and bent down to crawl through the low doorway. She groped her way in the darkness to where the coughing was coming from. Jim lay on his bed amid a pile of rugs, pillows and blankets with a dirty sheepskin flung over him. The dog sat down dutifully by his side. Jim's skin was sallow and flaky, and his hair and beard were longer than ever. Alice fetched him a mug of water from a pitcher he kept by his little camping stove. He sat up and drank a little. Alice touched his forehead. It was burning.

'You need to see a doctor, Jim,' she said.

He looked at her blankly, watching her lips move. She realised he hadn't heard what she said, so she pulled out her notebook and pencil to write down the word 'doctor'. Jim fixed his gaze on the book, and a flicker of recognition came over his face. He reached across and grabbed the book from Alice's hand. She offered him the pencil, thinking that he wanted to write something down for her, but he waved the pencil away and began to flick through the pages, more feverish than ever. When he reached the page where there was a drawing of the C-Bean Mark 2, he pointed at the page repeatedly and then at his chest. Alice peered at him with wide eyes as she came to a slow realisation … What? Could it be?

Alice did a quick mental calculation – if this *was* him, he must now be eighty-eight years old. She could hardly believe he had been living here right under her nose all this time – no wonder Alice always had felt like they'd always known each other! Old Jim was James Ferguson!

Alice looked harder at Jim's wrinkled face and a huge grin spread across her face. He started chuckling and was struggling to sit upright in bed. His laughter became louder and more raucous, which made him cough and cough until his face went blue. Then he seemed to forget how to take another breath, and his body went limp as he slumped back down onto the rugs.

'Jim, Jim, wake up!'

Spex joined in, barking and licking his owner's face. But Alice knew it was too late.

✠ ✠ ✠

The vicar held a funeral for old James Ferguson in the chapel a few days later. The summer term had just ended, and Alice asked if they could wait a day longer until her older sister Lori came back from boarding school on the mainland, so she could be there to give him a send-off too. It was a shame Dr Foster wasn't there, Alice thought, but just about everyone else turned out for it. Everyone was wearing black – including Lori, who usually made a point of only wearing fluorescent colours, although she still insisted on wearing her high-heeled shoes. Everyone except Lady Grange, that is. She decided Karla's black jeans and T-shirts were not suitable for a funeral so she washed her dark blue dress and put that on instead. Alice thought she looked very regal.

It was a sad affair and many of the villagers shed a tear or two, Alice included. But no one cried louder than baby Kit, who for some reason was very restless that day. Alice carried Kit in her arms all the way up to the graveyard in the procession to see the coffin being buried, and it occurred to her at that moment that it felt right for the last person to be born on St Kilda before its evacuation in 1930 to be the first to be buried there after the island's reinhabitation. It seemed nicely symmetrical. Even so, Alice was still having difficulty connecting the old man she had known all this time with the much younger friend she'd made called James in 1957. She still had so many unanswered questions, and now she felt she would never know the answers.

After everyone had trooped out of the little oval graveyard, Lori walked over to her sister.

'C'mon, Alice, don't make such a big deal of it. He was just some old man.'

Alice stared at her sister in disgust.

'OK, be like that, Ali. I'm going to the wake in the pub with Mum and Dad and the others. You'll have to give Kit his tea.'

Lori stomped off in her high-heeled shoes and left Kit and Alice in the graveyard. Alice realised she was just as upset about the loss of the C-Bean as she was for the loss of old Jim. Kit started crying again.

'Shhh, shhh, Kit, my little kittiwake, don't cry. He's up in heaven now,' Alice sobbed in her baby brother's ear, but she had no idea what heaven really was, and no way of knowing if it even existed. She just knew Jim's body was buried under that mound of fresh brown earth, alongside the babies from long ago. Maybe Jim himself was still in the past, maybe he was in the future, or perhaps he was right there with them – except that he was now invisible, just like the C-Bean. At least with Jim they'd put a marker where he could be found in the graveyard, unlike the C-Bean. With this thought Alice began to wander home.

After she'd finally settled Kit down for a nap, she lay on her bed and flicked through Jim's brown notebook once more, wondering if she'd made a mistake in not asking for it to be buried with him. She kept going back to the drawing he'd made of the C-Bean Mark 2, and was trying to make out what he'd written beside it, but it was a lot of strange maths. She began doodling a crude map of the island, adding the route they'd taken around the island by boat, the site of the nuclear weapons store, and the Amazon's house. She put down the pencil. She was beginning to doze off when there was a knock on her door.

'Come in,' Alice said sleepily.

'Hi Alice, are you OK? I just thought I'd pop round.' It was Charlie.

'Yeah, just feeling a bit sad, that's all.'

'I know something that will cheer you up.' Charlie seemed quite fired up for some reason, and was wandering around the bedroom beating his right fist into his other hand like it was a baseball glove.

'What's that?' Alice asked, yawning.

'Just a minute.' Charlie knocked on the window to attract someone's attention, then beckoned them to come inside.

Within seconds, Sam J and Sam F burst into Alice's bedroom and shouted in unison: 'We've found something. A secret cave. Under the gun.'

'Really?'

'Yes, and that's not all. We think the C-Bean's down there.'

The C-Bean's disappearance had been the source of much speculation on the island among the grown-ups, who had never known an item so large go missing, even in the wildest St Kildan storm. A week after it disappeared, they registered it with the Hebridean police as 'stolen', but the police made no progress investigating either that or the other disappearance on the island, namely Karla Ingermann. The detective on the case suggested the two disappearances might be linked, which made Alice think her hunch about Karla interfering with the C-Bean was right. But knowing the C-Bean's new-found ability to make itself invisible, she clung on to the hope that it was just a matter of time before they found it again.

But it was not quite how Alice imagined. After Jim's funeral, the two Sams had gone down to the jetty to mess about by the old gun emplacement. The gun was permanently pointed out to sea, trained on the horizon. It had been waiting to be fired ever since it was put there at the end of the First World War, unused for a century, waiting for an enemy attack. In the absence of a playground, to the island children it was a robust piece of play equipment that had led to endless imaginary games.

Once Alice had got the two seven-year-old boys to calm down and tell their story properly, she found out that during the course of their game that day, Sam F and Sam J had discovered they had somehow worked the gun's rusted bearings loose and they began to rotate it. When they had managed to turn the gun halfway round, so that it was pointing inland towards the chapel, they discovered that the turning motion was actually a mechanism that opened up a secret chamber beneath the gun mounting itself. When they climbed down into the chamber, they were convinced the C-Bean was down there, but they couldn't make it open.

'Alice, you have to come NOW and see,' they implored – as if she needed convincing. Alice was already bundling the sleeping Kit into his buggy. She put Jim's notebook in her pocket, and let the Sams lead the way, running and skipping with excitement, down to the headland, with Alice and Charlie taking turns to drag Kit's buggy down the rough grassy street behind them.

'Do Edie and Hannah know?' Alice asked as they went past their house.

'No – shall we get them to come down too, do you think?'

'Well, it's only fair,' Alice pointed out, and knocked on the door of her other two classmates.

Edie opened the door. She looked a bit glum.

'Hi Alice.'

'Get your boots and coats on and come with us, the boys have got something to show us apparently.'

James Ferguson's wake was still going strong when they passed the pub, and no one noticed when all the island children went past, heading for the gun emplacement late that afternoon.

Sam J ran on ahead and stopped at his house to get a torch, while Sam F fetched his walkie-talkie set from next door. The two of them sprinted the final hundred metres, and even from this distance Alice could see that a large dark hole had opened up in the ground beside the gun.

The children all stood round, peering down into the chasm below. Alice made sure she'd secured the brake on Kit's buggy. There was a rusty iron ladder hooked over the metal rim of the chamber.

'You first, Alice,' the Sams said in a hushed tone.

'Why me?' she enquired, biting her lip.

'Because you're the one who'll know how to make it work. Here, take this, and this.'

They handed her the torch and one half of the walkie-talkie set. Alice remembered using it when they were trying to escape from the Amazonian rainforest. Despite being right here on St Kilda, this moment seemed much more thrilling and dangerous.

✠ ✠ ✠

Alice worked her way carefully down the ladder, the torch and the walkie-talkie tucked under one arm and her heart beating fast. The handrails were damp and there was a metallic smell. When she stepped off at the bottom, she could see a dark cubic object looming, but it seemed to be wrapped in polythene. Was this really their C-Bean? She looked up and could see the silhouettes of several heads leaning over the hole above. The floor of the cave was puddled with seawater. Alice flicked on the torch and waded across to the C-Bean. She started to pull at the polythene sheeting. Beneath the layers of plastic, the surface of the C-Bean was mottled and grey, perhaps because it was going mouldy in this damp, airless environment.

'Charlie, come down, but be careful, it's a bit slippery.'

While Charlie descended into the chamber, Alice ran her hands over the C-Bean's walls until she could feel the access panel, then pressed to make it open. It was a bit stiff and in the end she had to use the pencil from her pocket to loosen it. When she shone the torch into the recess, a puzzled look came over her face – instead of the digital LED buttons and the slot for a cardkey there was just a large manual switch, like a power overrider. Below the recess with the switch was an empty shallow metal drawer. Alice slid the drawer in and out, but it didn't do anything.

'Come over here, Charlie – this is really odd.'

Charlie examined the drawer and then looked at the handle.

'Looks just like the master switch at the Evaw plant they used to get the whole thing fired up and working.'

'That's just what I was thinking, Charlie! But why's it different? Who's changed it?'

'Dunno. But look at this, Alice!'

Charlie had pushed aside more of the polythene to reveal a somewhat faded notice taped over the door itself. They both read the words out loud in unison: 'War Office Property. Unauthorised Entry Forbidden.' There was a date scrawled along a dotted line underneath and someone's signature, but it had got wet at some point and they couldn't read what it said.

'What do you think happened, Charlie? Shall we try and get inside?'

'No idea. Looks like it's been here a while.'

Alice gingerly lifted the switch. It made a loud grinding noise, and it took both of them to force it all the way up, but finally there was a small whirr and a click, as if some gears had slotted into place. Charlie peeled the sign off the door, and they waited, but nothing happened. The door remained resolutely shut.

'Talk to it, Alice – you know, like you did before.'

Alice stroked the side of the C-Bean and cooed softly, 'Come on baby, open the door for me, it's Alice'.

There was a low buzzing sound and then a crackle. A child's voice said, 'What's happening? Can we come down? We're getting bored up here!' Alice realised it was just Sam F on the walkie-talkie.

Charlie flicked on the other walkie-talkie and reported 'We can't get it working. You might as well stay up there for now. Sorry, guys. Over.'

Hannah's voice called down, 'Sing the sea shanty, Alice'.

Alice started humming the tune, but she didn't hold out much hope. She ran her hands over the C-Bean's surface, but it didn't change colour at all. And it had a rougher texture than she remembered. There was something not right about it, like it had been interfered with in some way, and she felt sure it could no longer respond to her.

Charlie, meanwhile, took the torch and started exploring the rest of the cave.

'Hey, Alice – look over here!'

The torch beam lit up one corner of the cave to reveal a tunnel. They had to walk one behind the other because it was quite narrow. It appeared to have been blasted out of the rock and a rope handrail was fixed at intervals to the wall at waist height. Alice walked along the tunnel in silence. She couldn't seem to get out of her mind the image of James's wrinkled old face lying in his underground house. They emerged after a few minutes in a vast concrete-lined room with a metal walkway around the edge and in the centre a large tank full of water. After a few seconds, a set of overhead lights flickered on, perhaps triggered by their movement. Charlie and Alice both froze.

The water in the tank glowed green, as if lit from below. At first Alice thought it was empty, but then she noticed standing upright in the water were hundreds of thin metal rods that had been slotted into the compartments of a submerged steel basket, like cutlery in a dishwasher. At the far end of the pool there were several larger cylindrical items, also submerged. Alice could hear an alarm going off faintly, and noticed three red warning lights flashing on the wall opposite.

Charlie looked incredulous. 'What is this? Do you think our dads know about it?'

On the wall just behind them Alice noticed the same ominous yellow-and-black danger symbol that James had shown her in the top secret file, and her heart started pounding.

'I don't know, but look, I think this stuff is radioactive, Charlie. If the alarm's gone off, it must be leaking or something. We should get out of here, just in case. I've got a horrible feeling we've stumbled across the nuclear waste dump that James suspected was on St Kilda all along.'

'Yep, bet you're right – come on, then,' Charlie replied with a grim look on his face.

They walked quickly back to the first chamber where the C-Bean was standing. They paused in front of it for a moment before climbing the ladder.

'You know why we can't get inside it, don't you Charlie?' Alice asked in a quiet voice.

'Why?'

'Because this is not our C-Bean.'

All the next day Alice couldn't stop thinking about the luminous underground tank with the strange cylinders in it. She had to let James know what they'd found under the gun emplacement. It was so frustrating to see the other C-Bean standing there when they were unable to get inside. She either needed to get their own C-Bean back, or get the other one working. If only Jim was still alive, she could maybe ask for his help. She felt like she could hear the alarm ringing constantly in her head as if it was saying, 'Do something!' Charlie thought they should tell the adults what they'd found. But Alice stubbornly clung to the hope that she could think of another way to deal with it.

After tea that evening she walked up to Jim's underground house to try and coax Spex out to eat something, and maybe even come back to her house. Ever since Jim had died, the dog just wouldn't come out and sat by the bed whimpering. She took a plate of warm chicken to entice him, a bowl of fresh water and a cardboard box.

'Spex, where are you?' Alice called as she stepped inside the dwelling.

She found him curled up asleep on the dirty sheepskin rug. He roused himself and half wagged his tail when he saw Alice. While he ate the food, Alice started putting Jim's things in the cardboard box, as her mum had suggested. There was only one item of furniture other than the bed, a large oak sea chest against one wall. It was black with age and had carved panels on all four sides. Alice opened the lid and looked inside. There was a musty smell coming from the blankets laid on top. She lifted them out. Underneath, to her surprise she found the ornate candlestick she recognised as Lady Grange's. Beside it lay a bible, and beneath that, wrapped in brown paper, was the top secret government file that she'd given him in 1957, now somewhat tattered.

She closed the lid of the chest and was about to leave with the box and the dog. She looked around the dwelling one last time, and felt she should make Jim's bed. She smoothed the rugs and quilts, then picked up the pillow to plump it and noticed a leather-bound notebook lying under it on the mattress. It looked exactly the same as the one she had, but this one had a red cover instead of a brown one. She opened it to look at the first page. It was a diary of sorts, and the first entry was 1st June 1957. James must have started another one when he realised the brown one had gone missing. Alice laid the notebook in the cardboard box with the other things and took it all home.

Her house had developed a strange unsettled atmosphere over the last few days. Her dad was ill in bed. Alice couldn't remember that ever happening before, and it was making her mum really stressed. When Alice walked into the kitchen, her mum was on the phone to Evaw's head office in Edinburgh.

'Yes, I know, Les, but the odd thing is Dr Cheung and my husband both have the same symptoms. I know they have been under a lot of stress lately, but the sickness is getting worse, not better. I really think someone needs to fly over and do a health and safety check on the plant. Perhaps there's something wrong. Mmm. OK. I'll call you again tomorrow, Les. Is 9am OK?' Mrs Robertson put down the phone and sighed.

'Mum, is Dad going to be OK? I'm really worried!' Alice whispered.

'I sincerely hope so, sweetheart. I see you persuaded Spex to come back. Maybe that will cheer your dad up. Did you get Jim's things? Was there much in that hovel of his?'

'Just his mother's bible and a candlestick, but I think I know who it belongs to. And this old red notebook. Is it OK if I go round to Charlie's for a bit? I want to tell him something.' Alice asked, stuffing the notebook into Karla's bag.

'Yes, so long as you're back by 9.'

Alice loved the long summer evenings on St Kilda, when the sky just faded to a dull glow but never went completely dark, and it was warm enough not to need a coat when you went outside. But tonight, the greenish glow on the horizon only reminded her of the weird tank in the cave. She looked across at the gun silhouetted on the headland and the roof of the Evaw office nearby. Something suddenly occurred to her and a feeling of dread shuddered through her. What if their fathers had been exposed to a radioactive leak coming from the cave? What if that was what was making them sick?

Alice ran the rest of the way, burst into Charlie's house without knocking, and darted through the living room where his mum was reading a book and into Charlie's room, panting for breath.

Charlie looked up from his computer. 'Alice, whatever's the matter?'

'Radiation sickness! That's what they've got Charlie! That chamber's leaking right next to Evaw's shed, that's why they're ill. Look it up on the Internet – I bet you I'm right!'

Charlie peered at his laptop screen and they scrolled through a list of symptoms. Vomiting, fatigue, headaches, dry cough, burning, rapid heartbeat, hair loss …

'Wow, Dad's got all of these. Mum's going crazy. He's so ill he's in bed.'

'So's mine. What are we going to do? Maybe Jim was affected too. He had the same cough and high temperature, you know. I think that tank we found in the cave may only be the tip of the iceberg – what if they've stored loads more in other caves or under the sea out there in the bay, just like James predicted?' Alice blurted out, her eyes wide and her breath uneven. She paused and pulled something out of her pocket.

'And look, I found this, Charlie.'

Alice handed Charlie the red notebook and he starting flicking through the pages.

'Whose is this?'

'I found it under Jim's pillow. For all I know he's probably written stuff down about the radioactive waste in here. It's some sort of record of his theories and inventions - look at all the diagrams and calculations, Charlie.'

The two children pored over the pages. The dates of the entries were entirely random – one page was from the 1950s, the next 1971, then 2000, then back to the mid-1960s. Suddenly Alice caught sight of a detailed drawing of the power lever they'd seen on the other C-Bean.

'Hey, Charlie, look at that!'

The next page was a sketch of the metal drawer, which James had labelled 'Instant mailboat'. Charlie scratched his head.

'Maybe the C-Bean in the cave is a prototype that James built after he'd seen our one. That would explain why it's different. The War Office must have found out he was building it and confiscated it from him – which is why it's down there covered in notices and polythene!' Alice was lost in thought for a moment, staring at the sketch. Then she gasped and clapped her hand over her mouth.

'Charlie, I think I know what the drawer is for! We can use it to communicate with him.'

'How come?' Charlie asked, popping a piece of chewing gum into his mouth and offering Alice some.

'No thanks. Don't you remember, in the olden days people on St Kilda used to send messages to the mainland in miniature waterproof containers called *mailboats* when they needed help. It's James' idea of a joke, calling it an "instant mailboat"! I reckon he was trying to invent a device that would let you send a message instantly from one time to another in an emergency.'

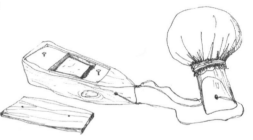

Alice looked at her watch. It was almost 9 pm, but she felt there was no time to lose.

'Charlie, we need to try it right now. This *is* an emergency. Maybe James can help us find a way to make our dads better.'

Alice tore a page from the red book and wrote a note on it addressed to James, telling him that their fathers were sick, and that they thought they'd found the nuclear waste dump that he'd been looking for in a hollowed-out chamber beneath the gun. She signed and dated it, Friday 27th July 2018.

They slipped out of the back door without Charlie's mother noticing, and headed down to the gun emplacement. The mechanism was very stiff, but between them they managed to rotate the gun towards the chapel and open the hatch just enough to be able to squeeze through and climb down.

They had forgotten to take a torch, so they had to grope their way towards the C-Bean in the dark. Alice reached it first and felt her way to the access panel and opened the little door.

'Right – let's give it a go, Charlie.'

Charlie pulled the lever back down to its starting position and Alice slid open the metal drawer, placed the folded note inside and closed it again.

He lifted the handle, and they could both hear the gears whirring and clicking into place like the previous time. Then they stood in the dark and waited. Water was dripping from the roof of the cave onto their heads. Alice shivered. Silence.

'OK, let's come back early in the morning and check it,' said Charlie.

They were halfway up the ladder when there was a muffled scraping sound, followed by the faintest of clicks.

'Did you hear that?' Alice squeaked. She jumped back down off the ladder and stumbled across to the C-Bean. She felt inside the access panel and her heart skipped a beat.

'The lever – it's moved, Charlie – I was right!'

'Well, open the drawer then and see.'

Alice pulled the drawer and felt inside. The letter was still there. Disappointed, Alice picked it up and then suddenly realised it was not her note. This one was in an envelope, and it was sealed up.

✠ ✠ ✠

It was almost too dark to read the letter when they got above ground. Charlie closed up the cave entrance, trying to make as little noise and possible, but even so Mr Butterfield heard them as he was heading for the pub.

'What are you two kids doing out this late? You shouldn't be playing with that gun,' he shouted.

'I left my sweater here earlier,' lied Charlie.

They waited until he was out of sight and then Alice tore open the envelope. It was unmistakably James's handwriting.

My dear Alice
So pleased you worked out how to operate the mailboat feature! The rest of my C-Bean experiment has been a bit of a disaster so far, but I'm still working on it. Thanks for the tip-off about the nuclear waste dump. I've got a contact now who's quite high up in government. They told me St Kilda is still on the list as a preferred waste site but so far no decision has been made as to whether they will actually use it. Rest assured, Alice, I will do my best to make sure they go with one of the other options that would be much less damaging.
Yours, James
PS I wonder if you could send me a few materials I need to get my C-Bean prototype up and running. I need ...

'Hey, Alice, what the hell do you think you're doing out here?' It was Lori, who had obviously been sent out to look for her. Alice could see her sister's fluorescent pink jeans approach them in the deepening twilight. She hid the letter behind her back and glanced at her watch. It was nearly ten o'clock.

'Mum's been getting worried. What have you got there? Let me see. Are you two writing love letters to each other, or what?' Alice could tell by Lori's tone of voice that she was being ridiculed. She passed Lori the letter, and was grateful James had omitted to date it.

'Where did you get this?'

'We found it ...' Alice faltered.

'... in Karla's office, among her papers,' Charlie butted in, covering for her.

'Why's it addressed to you then, Alice?' Lori was nothing if not persistent. 'And who's this James? Is he your "*boyfriend*"?'

'Shut up, Lori – it's a letter from a … scientist. I asked him to look into whether there's a possibility that it's a nuclear accident or some kind of radioactive leak that's making our dad and Charlie's dad ill, if you really want to know.'

Lori fell silent and read the note again.

'I see. Does Mum know about this scientist friend of yours?'

Alice shook her head. Lori stuffed James's letter into her back pocket.

'Well, we'd better go back and tell her you've been snooping around the German spy's office. You can't keep disappearing like this – it's freaking her out.'

'Lori, don't be mean. Think about it. Dad's sick. I just want to help, that's all.'

With that, Lori walked off. Alice rolled her eyes at Charlie, and they both followed Lori up through the village. Charlie peeled off at his house with a silent wave and a shrug, as if to say don't worry, it'll be OK. But Alice was fighting back tears of anger. She could feel them pricking in her eyes, and she swallowed hard before running to catch her sister up.

'Wait up, Lori – I've got something else to tell you.'

Lori wheeled round to face her, but instead her gaze fell on something unexpected behind Alice.

'What the …'

Alice turned and saw Lady Grange running half-naked towards them, locks of curly red hair flapping around her face. She tripped on a tuft of grass and fell over.

'Lady Grange, what on earth's the matter?'

The woman lay writhing on the ground, delirious and distraught, tugging at her clothes and hair. Alice ran back to help her to her feet.

'I had to get out of that box, Alice! It was too bright, and there were too many pictures. Get me the nurse! I need some more of her magic medicine. Where is Karla hiding? I need to hide too, or they'll find me. I know they will!'

'Lori, can you go and get Edie's mum? Tell her Lady Grange is ill again. She knows what medicine to give her. And bring a blanket.'

Lori scurried off in the dark, while Alice knelt down and stroked Lady Grange's hair to calm her down. She was puzzled – why did she mention Karla, and what did she mean by a 'box' – could she possibly have found the C-Bean?

'Do you know Karla? They've made me wear her clothes and live her life and I don't want to any more. I am not her!' Lady Grange implored.

'No, of course you're not Karla. Nobody said you were. It's OK, I understand.'

Alice left a pause, then asked gently, 'Lady Grange, what box are you talking about?'

Lady Grange pointed vaguely above the village. 'Up there! I couldn't get out. I was stuck inside it for hours, but no one came.'

Alice stared into the gloom at the silent mountain ridge. Could the C-Bean have returned to where it had been left in 1957, and Lady Grange had somehow found it when she was roaming around? Alice's heart was pounding, but she knew there was no way she could go and look until tomorrow. She could just make out two figures hurrying towards her.

'Come on now, dear, let's get you to bed. My, she's got a shocking temperature,' Edie's mum Jane said in her 'I'm-a-nurse' voice, wrapping a blanket around Lady Grange's shoulders and easing her up.

Lori stood a few feet away, biting her bright orange fingernails.

'Will she be all right?' Alice asked. 'She seems very confused.'

'Let's hope so. There are too many ill people on this island – it's enough to make us evacuate it all over again!' Edie's mum said emphatically. With that, she led Lady Grange away.

The two sisters walked back home in silence. Alice wanted to ask Lori to give the letter back, but she decided not to. Now there was a chance their C-Bean had reappeared, maybe there was no need.

✠ ✠ ✠

Alice was woken in the morning by her dad. When she opened her eyes she was convinced she must still have been dreaming, because he was fully dressed and looked completely well again. No redness on his face. Even his hair had grown back.

'Come on, sleepyhead. It's your favourite day of the week – Saturday! I've been up hours, already taken Spex for a walk, and your mum's come up with a plan for us to make up a picnic and all go for a family walk up Conachair in the sunshine.'

Alice hugged him and remembered the letter.

'Is Lori awake?'

'No. Why don't you go and wake her, and we'll all have breakfast?'

Alice crept into her sister's bedroom and nudged the sleeping hump of bedclothes.

'Hey Lori, guess what? Dad's well again!'

The hump spoke: 'Why'd you have to wake me to tell me that, you idiot? Since when was he ill?'

Alice frowned and went back to her room to get dressed. She needed to check for sure, so she ran down to Charlie's house and let herself in. They were all sitting round the table having breakfast – there was Dr Cheung, tucking into bacon and eggs and looking bright and breezy with a full head of hair, just like her own father.

'What can we do for you, Alice?' Mrs Cheung enquired. Charlie just winked at Alice.

'Nothing … see you later!' Next she ran to Edie's house. Edie opened the door.

'Did Lady Grange sleep here last night? Is she OK?'

'Lady Grange? No, why? She'll be in her room above the pub, as far as I know.'

'Of course. Silly me. See you later.'

'Wait, Alice. What's going on?'

But Alice skipped off back home for breakfast happy in the knowledge that, despite the risks, they'd successfully managed to reverse the damage that had been done to their island and their health.

✠ ✠ ✠

The two girls took it in turns to carry the picnic basket up to the ridge. It was a beautiful mild day, and Alice watched as her parents walked hand in hand up ahead, Kit bouncing on her father's back in a baby carrier, and Spex bounding backwards and forwards between them all, happy to be part of the family again. They picked a spot with the best view of the bay. Lori spread out the picnic blanket while Alice stared out to sea, completely distracted for a moment. She could see the Evaw machines anchored just below the surface, collecting wave energy, but in her mind's eye she could also still picture the mushroom cloud looming above the bay.

'What are you looking at? Aren't you going to help me, Alice?'

'Thank goodness.'

'What?'

'Nothing.'

'You're a weirdo, Alice.'

Later, while they were eating, Alice noticed something out of the corner of her eye. She felt sure she could see a brief flickering shape appear from time to time further down the mountainside, just on the flat piece of ground near the radar station. She kept her eye trained on the spot, and sure enough it happened again. This time the square shape was unmistakable – it was the C-Bean, no doubt about it. She hoped that no one else noticed the strange sight of it momentarily materialising and then disappearing again, like a mirage. She could hardly contain the surge of excitement welling up within her.

'Come on, Spex – chase me!'

She practically ran the last few hundred metres to the summit of Conachair, her arms outstretched like a little kid pretending to fly. Because in truth, that was how she felt.

On the way back down, Alice's mum made a suggestion.

'Why don't you two girls camp out tonight? The weather's fine – it'd be fun.'

Lori looked only vaguely interested, but Alice jumped at the idea, a secret ulterior plan already forming in her mind.

'Can we ask Charlie and Edie to come too?'

'Does Charlie have a tent?'

'Yes, he has a four-man one, actually.'

'I'm not sleeping in a tent with Charlie,' announced Lori.

'Well, why not let Charlie sleep in our two-man and you three girls can use his then,' said their mother, always ready with a solution. 'You could even take Hannah too, if Jane says she can, since there'd be room.'

'Can we camp over in Gleann Mor?' Alice asked nonchalantly, wrapping her arms around her father's waist. She wanted to gain them a bit more time away on this trip.

'Yes, you're both old enough now, I suppose – but take Spex with you, for protection,' advised Alice's dad, stopping to admire the view one more time. 'Just look at the wave machines from up here – don't they look fantastic! What an amazing achievement, Alice, don't you think?'

'Yes. We've changed history, Dad,' Alice said proudly, even though they were talking about two different things.

✠ ✠ ✠

Alice managed to grab two minutes alone with Charlie to tell him her plan. They were rolling up sleeping bags and stuffing them into drawstring sacks in his room. The others were down at the shop buying provisions.

'So, once the girls are asleep, we can creep back up to the place on the ridge where I saw the C-Bean, and I reckon we'd be back in the tent before they wake up.'

'It sounds a bit risky, but we can give it a go.'

'Please let's do it. I really need to find out if James is OK.'

'Well, we know he was OK, because he survived well into his eighties!' teased Charlie.

'You know what I mean,' Alice giggled, thumping him in the stomach.

✠ ✠ ✠

The expedition over to Gleann Mor went without a hitch, except that Edie was a bit grumpy about the whole thing. They were rewarded with a spectacular sunset. The whole valley was bathed in a peachy pink light, making their faces glow orange. In actual fact it was a bit chilly, so Charlie lit a campfire using barbecue coals in a tin tray, because there was no wood around to light a real one. Alice realised they'd pitched the tents near the stream she had drunk from the morning she woke there, cold and alone, in 1957. With their colourful tents, and having Spex with them this time for company, the place felt much less desolate. Lori started telling them made-up ghost stories while they warmed up the baked beans they'd brought and buttered some bread for tea. Alice looked like she was listening, but really she was remembering her own strange encounters in this valley, and about losing James there. When it was her turn to tell a story, she didn't need to make it up. But she realised it didn't have a proper ending.

'You can't end a ghost story like that,' objected Edie when Alice's voice trailed off with the words 'That's all'. 'The man can't just vanish and leave the girl wandering around all over looking for him. And anyway, how did he go off when his ankle was hurt?'

'Well, that's my story – it's someone else's turn now.'

After that they ate in silence. Charlie rinsed off the plastic plates in the stream and then went inside his tent. Spex followed him.

✠ ✠ ✠

Alice lay very still in her sleeping bag, listening to the other two girls dropping off to sleep. She didn't move a muscle until she was sure she could hear them making the kind of steady breathing patterns that meant they were sound asleep. She wriggled out of her sleeping bag without unzipping it and lifted the flap of the tent door she'd deliberately left open (so she could 'breathe', Alice had told them). Charlie had done the same, and she found him sitting on his sleeping bag, fully dressed and ready to go, his hand over Spex's muzzle so he wouldn't try to greet Alice. They moved away from the campsite and up the slope, without speaking a word until the dying embers from the campfire were just a pale orange dot.

'Did you bring your torch?' Alice whispered finally.

'Yep. Are we near the spot?'

'Not much further.' It was still not quite dark on the horizon to the west, and the remaining light made everything look as if it was different shades of blue. Just then, up ahead, Alice saw a much darker flicker, a straight edge, and then the vertical line was gone. Now she knew what she was aiming for.

'This way, Charlie.' They moved off the path and made their way diagonally across a large patch of thicker grass, Spex sniffing his way through the undergrowth. As they got closer, the glimpse of an edge turned into a steadier slab of black. The closer Alice got to it, the more substantial the C-Bean became, as if she was calling it into being with her very presence.

Suddenly, they were standing in front of it.

'It seems bigger, doesn't it?' Charlie whispered.

'Much,' Alice agreed, and touched it for the first time. She could swear it trembled, but it was probably her hand, not the C-Bean. The door opened and they both stepped inside.

Alice sat on the floor, stroking Spex and basking in the soft white light that emanated from every surface around her. For some reason she felt she was finally home. It was strange, when most of the time the C-Bean seemed to make her go anywhere *but* home. It was like something in her blood, her pulse even, was connected to this pod.

'Right, we haven't got all night. What's the deal?' Charlie paced impatiently in circles around her. His footsteps made something on the floor shift around. Alice noticed there were sheets of paper scattered on the floor, and started to gather them up. Someone had written pages and pages with a pale lilac felt-tip pen. The writing began small and neat, and became larger and more angry-looking and then it looked like the pen must have run out.

'Lady Grange. It must have been what she wrote when she was stuck inside here. Look at this, Charlie.'

'Can't we look at that later, Alice? There isn't time now.'

'OK, you're right. Let's go and find James – we still don't know why he wasn't in Gleann Mor when I went back for him.'

'So, chalk it up!'

Alice asked for a pen, and wrote very specifically on the wall in huge swirling writing: *28th July 1957, Gleann Mor, St Kilda, Scotland*, so that the C-Bean could be in no doubt about the place and time.

For no apparent reason, just before the command was acted upon, the C-Bean asked Alice for permission to perform a software update.

'What shall I say, Charlie?'

'It might add some useful new features – go for it!'

Alice gave her consent, and it announced in a dull monotone that it was adding two new patches, effectively upgrading it to a C-Bean Mark 4. There was a wavering sensation, when not only the C-Bean but even Alice's body and Charlie's too seemed to flicker and fragment slightly. She had never consciously experienced the dematerialisation process before, but this time it was a truly physical, and not entirely pleasant, sensation. It occurred to her that perhaps they shouldn't time travel too often, in case it did something bad to your insides.

It was most peculiar to step back out of the C-Bean in the very place where they'd pitched their camp earlier and find there was no longer anything there. No tents. No children. No campfire. And then the C-Bean itself did the oddest thing – in a matter of seconds, it vanished, leaving nothing on the ground except the cardkey. Spex sniffed it inquisitively. Even that looked slightly different, too. There was still a logo of a spinning globe on it, but it was black and rubbery.

'That's the updated C-Bean Mark 4 for you,' joked Charlie, and he picked it up out of the grass and tossed it to Alice. She examined the black card and then slipped it into her jeans pocket.

'What now?'

'We walk over to James's house.'

✠ ✠ ✠

They decided not to use Charlie's torch until they were inside the house, and what it revealed when they flicked it on was quite a shock – not only was James nowhere to be found, but his place had been ransacked. Everything had been turned upside down, and Alice knew immediately what the War Office men had been looking for. She imagined that James must have gone into hiding somewhere, and taken the file with him, since she knew he still had it in his possession the day he died. But it upset her when she caught sight of a navy blue box trampled on the floor, and found that Donald's medal had been taken. All that remained was the imprint of the cross in the red velvet.

Charlie was eating a biscuit he'd found in the kitchen cupboard.

'I think it's safe to say James has done a runner,' he said with his mouth full. Spex was sniffing around his ankles for crumbs. Then the dog seemed to latch onto another, stronger scent, and barked. He trotted out of the house and down the street.

'Let's follow him – seems like he's onto something,' Alice said, reluctant to return to the present just yet.

'In the pitch dark? What if we get caught by the army people you said were here?'

'It's midnight, Charlie, they'll all be fast asleep, and we won't make a sound.'

'OK. No barking, Spex,' Charlie hissed, his jaw tense.

Spex, silent and obedient, moved off at quite a pace, and Charlie was right – it was finally dark. The dog looked like he was heading towards the jetty at the bottom of the village. They both jogged to catch up with him. None of the houses had any lights on, but there was some washing hanging in a couple of the backyards. Alice realised that the nature conservationist team must have arrived. Spex carried on past the jetty and up the headland on the other side, stopping at the gun emplacement, wagging his tail and circling round it.

'You don't think …' Alice ventured.

'Could be.'

They shoved the barrel of the gun round towards the chapel. It moved with considerably more ease than in 2018, and the hatch opened without a sound. Spex was so excited that he almost fell into the hole. Charlie flicked on his torch and shone it on the ladder so Alice could climb down. He then handed her the torch and lifted the dog down to her, not wanting to risk leaving him above ground in case he started barking.

'James, are you down here?' Alice called out.

She surveyed the chamber while she waited for Charlie. Scattered all over the floor were half-eaten cans of food and a variety of tools. Spex picked through them, eating any morsels that he found. Propped against one wall were a number of sheets of metal next to something that looked like a half-built raft or base. It was obvious this had been James's laboratory where he was attempting to assemble his prototype C-Bean. There was a drawing with measurements written on it lying beside a box containing some kind of mechanical item, which Alice then recognised was the power switch. James had obviously ordered it from somewhere but had yet to incorporate it into his design. His undated note to her must have been sent from a time much later, when his homemade C-Bean was almost complete.

'Alice, it's not here,' Charlie said quietly.

'Huh?'

'The other chamber. I mean there's no way through. Look – the rock hasn't been touched.'

Alice flashed the torch beam across to where Charlie stood.

'They must have blasted out that chamber some time after 1957, then,' Alice mused.

'Well, anyway, he's not here, so let's go.'

They climbed back up the ladder, and then Alice remembered Spex. She went back down and found him curled up on a rough woollen sweater that had been dropped on the floor next to the tools.

'C'mon, Spex,' Alice coaxed, and tugged at James's sweater. The dog stood up and stretched. Alice saw something shiny on top of a piece of paper in the dent where the dog had been lying. She picked up the shiny object, which was warm from the dog's body. She turned it over in her hand. It looked just like the metal tag on a chain she'd once found in the Amazon's house, and was engraved with some information including those same initials Alice had noticed before – DCF. The piece of paper was a note from James.

'Charlie, give me the torch a minute.'

✠ ✠ ✠

My dear Alice

Glad you found your way down here. Sorry to disappoint you by not being here to meet you. As you can see, they have searched high and low for any incriminating evidence in my possession, but I've hidden it well, and so far they have not discovered this lab of mine, where as you can see I am now more or less living. Dad told me about it. He said they discovered the cave when they installed the gun up here towards the end of the First World War but it was a well-kept secret among the islanders. The only other person who knew about its existence was that Karla woman, but she's long since gone.

There's something I want you to do for me now, if you don't mind. It's about Dad. Remember how I told you that he was brought down in a seaplane in World War II? Well, some other information has come to light since I last saw you and, amazingly, it seems he must have crashed on St Kilda. Dad was trying to land in the bay at Gleann Mor but must have misjudged the landing and the wind direction somehow. The conservation people told me in the pub yesterday that they'd found human bones and wreckage in the valley there, so I'm convinced he didn't die instantly. They also found this dog tag there, in the Amazon's house, with his number, blood group and initials on it: DCF. So I know it was really him. Dad must have died there. I want you to take the C-Bean and go to the crash site in Gleann Mor and see if you can find him. I was trying to finish my C-Bean in time to go myself and rescue him, but it was more tricky than I thought, that's why I need you to go: the crash took place just after midnight on 29th July 1944. Good luck, Alice – I know this will mean as much to you as it does to me. Just make sure he lives, that's all I ask.

   JF

Alice gulped when she got to the last line. Charlie was reading it over her shoulder.

'That's tonight Charlie!'

'Looks like we've got our work cut out,' he said grimly.

'We better get out of sight of the village before we use the C-Bean,' Alice said thoughtfully, putting the dogtag in her pocket and feeling it make contact with the new black cardkey.

Charlie picked up James's sweater and they left the chamber in silence, leaning against the gun to close up the hatch and leave it just as they found it. Spex sensed a change in their mood and walked sombrely beside them. They avoided the army camp, climbing diagonally behind the village up to the ridge.

The radar station was locked up and in darkness, and Alice thought it was safe to summon the C-Bean on the adjacent spot where it had arrived once before. She looked at her watch. It was exactly midnight. She pulled the dogtag and cardkey from her pocket. Putting the dogtag around her neck,

Alice took a deep breath, held out the new cardkey and stood still.

She could hear Charlie sniggering to himself.

'What's so funny, Charlie?'

'What are you going to do next – say "Abracadabra"?'

'Erm … I don't actually know,' Alice answered, aware she was failing to see the funny side of things.

She closed her eyes and thought for a moment.

'Whoah – well, whatever you did, it's working!' Charlie spluttered.

Alice opened her eyes and the C-Bean stood before her. She flipped open the access door and slotted in the cardkey. The door opened and Alice stepped inside. Charlie threw James's sweater on the floor and Spex immediately lay down on it again.

'Right, we're going to need to take some things with us.'

Alice picked up the pen and began making a list on the wall, like she had done once before. It was strange to think that it was Donald who'd helped her carry the hamper of food and medicine out of the C-Bean to leave for the starving villagers back in 1851, and now here she was, making up an inventory of food and medicine to help Donald himself survive his own catastrophe.

'We might need crutches, Alice. James didn't say what his injuries were,' Charlie suggested.

Once they had assembled all the equipment they could think of in the middle of the C-Bean's floor, Alice announced their destination as before – *29/07/1944, 00.15, Gleann Mor.* The same destabilising feeling of being simultaneously fragmented and then rapidly put back together came over her, as the C-Bean recalibrated its time frame yet again to perform this mercy mission. Judging by the look on Charlie's face, he was feeling distinctly odd too.

Worse than this feeling of being physically rearranged was Alice's sense of dread at the prospect of what they might find when they stepped out of the C-Bean to confront the wartime carnage of Donald's crashed plane.

Alice's Blog #4

Sunday 29th July 2018

What an intense few hours! I never want to go through something like that again as long as I live. I didn't know what to expect when we left the C-Bean, but I think I was at least counting on a calm summer's night. Instead we found ourselves in the middle of the most horrendous storm. Stupid really, I should have thought of that — I mean, why else would Donald have crashed?

Anyway, Charlie and I struggled headlong into the wind and the rain with all the stuff, but it was pretty dark and we could hardly see anything. We were about to go back and ask the C-Bean for tarpaulins or some polythene sheets to keep everything dry when we heard a man's voice calling out in the darkness, obviously in a lot of pain.

I called out, 'Donald, is that you?' and tried to walk towards where the sound was coming from. I kept tripping over bits of the wreckage that were strewn everywhere on the hillside. Eventually we found him sheltering in a section of the fuselage that had landed in a gully. He was lying awkwardly, still wearing his leather flying jacket, with one leg propped up. I was no expert about what kind of condition he was in, but it didn't look great. There seemed to be blood everywhere, and his face was barely recognisable.

'What do we do?' I asked Charlie helplessly, but he just stared in shock. I gave Donald some water and some painkillers and he seemed to come to his senses a little. He wanted to know if we'd been in the plane too, and asked where the others were. I sent Charlie off to look around, but he came back looking worse than ever. He still hasn't told me half of what he saw last night. But as dawn came, I could see that it can't have been pleasant. In fact, I don't think I can write any more now. It's too upsetting.

One thing, though – Spex was instantly drawn to Donald. It was like he sensed the connection between Donald and James, or maybe he simply felt he should stay by a wounded man. 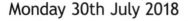 Mum once told us at school about these dogs in Belgium during the war who were trained to stay with injured soldiers until help came. Spex did exactly the same. So when he wouldn't come, I put Donald's dogtag around Spex's neck and left the two of them there.

Monday 30th July 2018

Charlie is traumatised and I don't know what to do. He won't get out of bed, and refuses to eat. He told his parents he had a vivid nightmare, but I know the awful truth. I stayed with him for ages this evening, just holding his hand. He says he wants to cry but he can't.

Lori's not much help. Of course she doesn't know what we went through – as far as she's concerned, Charlie was spooked by the ghost stories she told us, and she said in front of his parents that she thought he was being utterly pathetic. She's also on my case about the fact that when she and Edie woke up, Charlie and I were both in the same tent together. I couldn't leave him, though – he was shaking too much. So now Lori keeps taunting me about Charlie and me being in love, and how she's going to tell Mum and Dad. It's her that's being pathetic.

Tuesday 31st July 2018

I woke up in a panic this morning, really needing to know if Donald survived or not. What if he didn't? What if nobody saw the flare we let off in the hope that some plane would fly over looking for him? What if Spex left his side and wandered off? What if his leg went bad and he got that thing called gangrene where your leg has to be amputated? Should I have moved him or just left him where he was? It was a terrible thing to inflict more pain on a person even when you were trying to help them, but even getting him into the C-Bean was a huge feat. After that I let the C-Bean take over. I had barely enough energy to issue the command 'Diagnose please, treat injuries'. The C-Bean set to work, producing a hospital bed for him to lie on and showed me various little movies to explain to me how I needed to cut off the jacket and trousers and apply dressings to the wounds. Thankfully he hadn't lost so much blood that he needed to be given any extra. I don't think I could have done that. Poor Charlie couldn't cope at all and sat outside while all this was going on. I asked the C-Bean to put out a Mayday alert so that Donald would be picked up. He was even able to drink some hot chicken soup before I wrapped him all up in a load of blankets and then Charlie managed to put up a little army tent beside the C-Bean and helped me get Donald comfortable inside it.

I wanted to help Charlie feel better and stop worrying about Donald myself, so today I went down to the cave and sent James another note via the mailboat drawer. At first I thought that someone else had been down there, because the polythene that had been draped over the other C-Bean had gone, as had the sign that Charlie tore off the door. But then when I saw James had fixed a label to the switch mechanism, I realised that he'd somehow managed to keep his lab and his C-Bean project hidden from the War Office. The other chamber where the tank had been was also gone, and the rock wall was now untouched and looked just like it had in 1957. In my note I asked James if Donald was rescued OK, and how everything turned out. I couldn't believe it when he simply sent back a black and white photograph of his dad, in full military uniform, proudly wearing his Victoria Cross and also a second medal for his services. At his side was a small brown dog. James had scrawled on the back of the photo 'Dad and Spex, on the occasion of his medal ceremony, 30 November 1945, with love and thanks'. Charlie smiled when he saw it. He even got out of bed this evening and ate dinner at the table with his mum and dad. Progress!

Wednesday 1st August 2018

In all the events of the past few days, I forgot to say what happened with the C-Bean Mark 4. It turned itself invisible again when we arrived back in front of Charlie's tent, and I just put the new cardkey in my pocket. But then disaster struck because the next day Mum washed all our clothes from camp, and the cardkey accidentally went in the washing machine. I have no idea if it is waterproof or not, but ever since then it's been pulsing alternately hot and cold - one minute it feels like a lump of burning coal, and the next it's like holding a lump of freezing liquid nitrogen. Well that's probably exaggerating a bit, but either way, you can't bear to touch it. Charlie thinks we should wait a few days to see if it recovers, and then try and use it again. For now I have hidden it in the drawer by my bed along with James's brown notebook and Lady Grange's sheaf of notes.

I still have no idea what happened to Lady Grange while she was inside the C-Bean. I've asked her but she doesn't seem to remember. All I have are the sheets of paper she wrote in lilac ink, but I can't read most of it, and the bits I can seem to be mostly her recreating the letters she wrote when she was imprisoned on St Kilda in the past.

There are a lot of things I can't read in James' notebooks either, because James's handwriting is so bad or it's just too difficult to understand, but some strange things have come to light about the time before he came back to live on St Kilda. Charlie's got the red notebook at the moment — he says he wants to read it properly and check some facts. So far he says he's sure that it was James who was nominated for a Nobel Peace Prize in 1977, for his anti-nuclear warfare work — he wrote about how excited he felt the day he received the letter telling him he'd been selected! As far as we can tell he was working for some sort of government computer project after that, about time-coding. Judging by the entries written during the 1990s, he was living somewhere in Germany and employed by a company there to solve potential Millennium Bug glitches in their computer systems. It seems he was also the guy who invented a material called Obsidon — he wrote pages of formulae about it. There is something that struck me as weird, though — he stuck in an article from the Scottish Herald dated January 2003. It was a photo of James with a caption underneath asking people to come forward if they could identify this man. Apparently there was a warrant out for his arrest, and he was accused of causing the fire at that factory in China where they were manufacturing Obsidon. So did James go AWOL like Karla? Is that where all the money that old Jim donated came from? Is that why he came back to St Kilda to hide in the underground house?

Alice was dreaming that she was choking. Something bitter and hot was burning the back of her throat. When she forced open her eyes, the room was filled with smoke and intense heat. Then she noticed flames coming from the drawer by her bedside where the C-Bean key was kept. She scrambled out of bed and raised the alarm.

'Mum, Dad, Lori – the house is on fire, quick, wake up!'

She ran to Kit's cot and lifted him out, still asleep. The smoke was making her eyes stream. Her parents were groping their way across the room towards her, half awake and coughing. Lori stood in the bedroom doorway like a statue, unable to take in what was happening. Alice grabbed her by the sleeve and pushed her into the kitchen. Alice's dad opened the back door and they all tumbled out into the cold night air, panting and gasping for breath.

Smoke was pouring out of the house now. Through Alice's bedroom window they could see the first flames take hold. Alice's mum took Kit and shouted, 'Mike, get the hosepipe from round the back! Alice, go and get help!'

'What about all our stuff?' wailed Lori, sobbing.

Alice ran blindly down the village street, knocking on every door she passed, not even stopping to explain why she was waking them all in the dead of night. They would find out quickly enough – the flames were now visible from a hundred paces. Their whole house was on fire!

When she reached the pub at the other end of the village, she turned and saw a surging mass of people half walking, half running up the main street in their night clothes, all carrying buckets and blankets into the cloud of smoke, to try and extinguish the blaze. Alice could hear Mr McLintock revving up his truck to bring the water hose. She pushed open the door of the pub, ran up the stairs to Lady Grange's room and flung herself on her bed in floods of tears.

Lady Grange rolled over and squinted at her.

'Whatever is the matter, child?'

'They key to the box you found on the mountain, it's made my house catch fire, Lady Grange. What shall I do? It's all my fault!'

✠ ✠ ✠

Once the blaze had been brought under control, some of the men ventured inside the house to try and retrieve any items that weren't already burned or damaged. The fire hadn't reached as far as the living room or her parents' bedroom, but it did appear that it must have started in Alice's room, just as she feared. The family decamped to Edie's house, but Alice was inconsolable. However much anyone said it wasn't her fault, she stubbornly maintained that it was. Never had she needed the C-Bean so much as now – to be able to correct the effects of time. It felt so unfair that she had been able to deal with Donald's injuries, the nuclear dumping, their dads' radiation sickness and even stop the babies from dying, but she didn't know how to change things in her own life. All she wanted to do was return things to a time before the fire happened, but since the C-Bean's cardkey appeared to have been not only the cause of the disaster but also consumed in it, she now had no means of getting the C-Bean back.

'You can't change the way things are, Alice – it's just something that's happened, and everyone's safe, no one was hurt. Think of it like that.' Edie was taking a more philosophical approach to consoling Alice, who was lying on Edie's bedroom floor watching Kit playing with some building blocks.

'I suppose you're right.' Alice made a tower out of the blocks and the baby knocked it down and laughed. She stroked his fine red hair and he looked at her with his big blue eyes as if he could read her mind.

'I just feel so guilty, Edie. I should have realised there was something wrong with that Mark 4 cardkey when it started getting all hot. I should have thought that it could catch fire. Why did I put it next to my bed? And now James's notebook has been destroyed too.'

'It's not important, Alice. Anyway, the red one is safe at Charlie's house. Don't blame yourself.'

'Lori still blames me.'

'Just ignore her – she'll get over it. She seems pretty happy about the idea of you all going to stay at your grandparents' flat in Liverpool, since it means she can go on a massive shopping spree there and buy loads of new clothes.'

'That's another thing, Edie. I really don't want to go on this trip to Liverpool. I mean I want to see Granny and Gramps, but I'd rather they came here.'

'Well, there's no more room in our house.'

Alice's parents had decided they would take a holiday for the rest of August with her grandparents in Liverpool, while the work was done to rebuild their own house. The plan was to 'get everything back to normal', as Mrs Robertson put it, by the start of September, before the school term was due to start. Charlie's parents needed to go back to Hong Kong to visit his grandfather who was not well, so it had been decided that Charlie would also go with the Robertsons to Liverpool. The following morning, Alice's dad would be down at the jetty, overseeing the delivery of a whole load of building materials and replacements for their lost possessions that were due to arrive on the ferry.

Alice sighed. She suddenly felt utterly exhausted and realised that Edie was right – no one was hurt, and that was what really mattered. Plus, she still had the red notebook.

She crawled into her sleeping bag and was lulled to sleep by Kit's wordless baby talk. A little later, her dad stuck his head round the door to check on them.

'Everything OK, Edie?'

'Sort of.'

'She'll feel better in the morning when we get on that ferry. Thanks for being such a good friend to Alice. I'll be back to put Kit to bed in a sec.'

✠ ✠ ✠

Alice woke early and slipped out of bed. She grabbed a piece of paper and a pencil and walked down to the gun emplacement wearing her wellies and Edie's old dressing gown. Alice leaned on the barrel of the gun to write, then when she was done she moved the gun through ninety degrees and disappeared underground, reappearing a few moments later holding a small package.

It was starting to rain. Alice walked briskly back up the street to Charlie's and knocked on his bedroom window. All she knew was that the package was addressed to her in James's handwriting and contained more than just a single sheet by way of a reply. Charlie pulled back his curtain and smiled. He was still in his pyjamas. She waved the package at him and let herself in by the back door. They sat on Charlie's bed and tore open the package.

The first part was a short note written in pencil on a scrap of paper.

Dear Alice

I am so sorry to hear about your fire. It must have been awful for you.

I think in the circumstances there are some things you ought to know, things that I have only just found out myself as a result of asking you to save my father's life.

During his recuperation in military hospital, they encouraged him to write down his life story as part of his rehabilitation. As soon as I learned that your rescue mission to 1944 had been a success, I went to visit him in Glasgow, and he entrusted his memoir to me, saying he didn't want anyone to read it, since he had written things down that he had told no one else. I enclose Dad's memoir for you to read – it's incomplete but it will help explain a few things to you, as it did for me too. It has certainly helped me progress my own work, and to this end I am sure you will be delighted with the item contained in the box I have also enclosed here. Be sure to read it all the way through before you open the box, Alice!

Yours truly,

James

The memoir was written in small, neat old-fashioned handwriting on seven or eight sheets of blue airmail paper, by someone with a lot of time on his hands. As soon as Alice spotted the words 'Karla' and 'traitor' on the first page, her heart jumped. She scanned the pages rapidly, and as she finished each one, she handed it to Charlie to read. After half an hour she came to the end, her mind spinning as she waited for Charlie to get through the last page.

'So that's why it disappeared! Can you believe it – Karla took our C-Bean remotely using her laptop, once she'd mended it!' Alice exclaimed.

'Yeah, what a crafty operator, nicking the spare parts she needed from the stores at the Wireless Station while the army thought she was a Prisoner of War employed to decode any German messages they picked up. How sneaky is that?'

'I know. Donald must have been so angry when he found out and then they didn't believe him. I did wonder if it was Karla interfering, actually, but I didn't know why,' Alice admitted. 'She must have been more desperate than we realised to get back to her own time. No wonder she tried to attack Donald and me with a knife! But I don't understand why she sent the C-Bean back to us like that. Maybe she *is* on the island somewhere.'

'Nah. He says she vanished on 21st July, which is a few days before Lady Grange found it again here, so I reckon she returned it the same way she stole it – remotely – but she must have had to make some dodgy adaptations to it. I'm sure that's why the Mark 4 cardkey caught fire.'

'I think you're right, Charlie. Remember when I left 1918 in the C-Bean and there was a recording of Karla trying to control it, and the C-Bean said something then like 'Activating Remote Override'. Do you think she summoned it back once she'd mended the laptop and then engineered the whole Mark 4 upgrade thing then?'

'Dunno. But it's all toast now.'

Alice looked downcast.

'There's one thing, Charlie – I feel really bad about not going back to see Donald like I promised before they evacuated the island in 1930. He sounds so disappointed in the memoir.'

'Yeah, but Alice, think about it – that part hasn't happened yet. It's still in your future. You can still go.'

'How, exactly? Even if we could get the C-Bean back, which we can't, we're leaving for Liverpool later today on the ferry and we won't be back till the start of September. They leave St Kilda for good at the end of August, remember?'

Neither of them spoke for a few minutes. Charlie started packing his things to take to Liverpool. Alice stared out of the window at the rain beating down. She pictured Donald all those years ago in 1930, waiting for her down by the jetty, trying to delay the moment when he boarded the ferry in case she turned up.

'Hey, you can open the gift James sent now!' Charlie reminded her. Alice sniffed and unwrapped the package. It was the dark blue medal box. Inside, rolled in a soft white cloth, was a flat object. She felt it through the cloth. It wasn't cross-shaped, and it was too big to be Donald's dog tag. Alice unrolled the cloth, and what fell out stunned them both – it was a cardkey to the C-Bean Mark 3.

'Wow. How on earth … Karla?'

'Who knows where that came from?'

'Anyhow, it's not much good to us now,' Alice said forlornly, fingering the hologram logo of the globe on the cardkey.

'Unless … Look, Alice, look what's happening!' Charlie began.

She looked down and noticed that as she ran her fingers over the globe, it started spinning, and when she put the card down the spinning stopped a few seconds later. She traced the outline of the globe again, and this time a faint outline of the C-Bean began to appear in the room beside them.

'Do you think it will still work now it's a C-Bean Mark 4, Charlie?'

'Dunno. We could try.'

'Come on, let's go now,' Alice blurted. 'We haven't got much time!'

Alice ran to the schoolyard clutching the cardkey, with Charlie trailing after her with his mobile phone in his hand. There was a low mist hanging over the bay and it was raining hard. They were both still in their pyjamas, but it didn't seem to matter. She took shelter in the chapel porch, and started running her fingers over the hologram and singing the sea shanty softly under her breath. The outline of the C-Bean flickered into being, like a darker, thicker patch of mist in front of her, and then faded.

'I can't make it stay, Charlie!'

'Let me try.' He took the card from her, and she stepped out into the yard, moving nearer to the outline as it emerged. She touched the smooth sides, and the dark surface seemed to get firmer and steadier. She stretched her arms out wide, touching its suede-like surface, and pressed her cheek against the wall, as if she was holding it. Her warm breath was mingling with the mist, which was starting to envelop her, becoming a dense fog. It was so thick that Alice could hardly breathe. She had her eyes open but all she could see was whiteness. She could no longer feel the wall of the C-Bean and dropped to the ground with disappointment. It wasn't until that moment that she realised she was inside.

The walls gradually hardened over, and the mist cleared to reveal a recess in the wall that contained a pile of clothes. Alice picked them up and examined each item. They looked like something her grandmother might have worn as a child – a rough cotton blouse, a hand-knitted cardigan, thick socks, brown leather shoes and a pinafore dress made out of a beige tweedy fabric. Without thinking, she changed out of her pyjamas into the outfit, just as Charlie opened the door and stepped inside. The C-Bean seemed to register his presence too, because another set of clothes appeared in his size, also a little old-fashioned.

'You'll be pleased to know the cardkey's gone in OK,' he reported to her as Alice handed him the clothes.

'Erm … what are these?' he asked.

'Looks like the C-Bean has plans for us.'

There was a loud rap on the door. Alice looked at Charlie with a start. Charlie was pulling the shirt over his pyjama top when the door opened.

Lori stepped inside and stood with hands on hips, staring at their odd attire.

'What's going on with you two? Is this some kind of secret fancy dress club? Whatever you're up to, it's not what this classroom's supposed to be used for! Does Mum know you're in here?'

Alice and Charlie looked at each other.

'She'd better come with us,' Charlie mumbled.

Alice nodded and another set of clothes appeared in Lori's size. Charlie handed them to her. The door closed behind her.

'I'm not wearing these – you've got to be kidding. Look, this is ridiculous, what's going on?'

But Alice wasn't listening to her protests. Instead she just whispered a date and time that neither Charlie nor Lori could quite hear.

The C-Bean shuddered, rocked and then seemed to melt away. They found themselves standing on the foredeck of a ferry steaming into Village Bay. The ferry sounded its horn and within minutes the passengers around them were disembarking onto St Kilda's jetty. Alice followed along after them, and noticed a newspaper that had been left on one of the wooden benches. She picked it up and handed it to Lori, pointing to the date at the top of the page – 4th August 1930. Lori's eyes flashed with confusion and humiliation, but Alice could also sense her sister's excitement. She studied Lori for a moment. Maybe because her pinafore dress was a bit too short and showed her knobbly knees, she seemed much younger than sixteen, Alice thought, more like a kid.

'Come on, you'll get used to it, Lori,' she laughed. 'Think of it as an unusual school trip. We're going to pay Old Jim's dad a visit. It'll be fun.'

Alice and Charlie strode off the boat onto the jetty with Lori lagging behind in a wake of questions.

'Do Mum and Dad know about this, Alice? I mean about going back in time? How many times have you done this? How did you even know about it?'

'Oh, we've only done it a few times,' Alice answered casually. 'I don't know why, but right from the start I seemed to be the one that just knew how the C-Bean worked, perhaps because I found it first.'

They headed up the village towards James's house. Alice knew which one it was straightaway because she could see the branches of the little elm tree swaying in the wind in the backyard. Lori was open-mouthed, taking everything in. The islanders were obviously preparing for their imminent evacuation – bundles of their belongings were being packed into trunks and wooden crates all the way up the village street. A couple of men were pushing handcarts down to the jetty to load some of them onto the day's ferry – in fact more things seemed to be leaving the island than arriving.

As the three children approached the Fergusons' house, they could see a man moving boxes through the doorway of the Post Office next door.

He turned to face them, and then straightened up, with a puzzled look on his face that said, 'Do I know you?' He was wearing a postman's hat and a badge that said 'D Ferguson, Postmaster, St Kilda'.

'Hello, Donald,' Alice spoke. 'It's me, Alice – remember?'

A smile spread across his face as he looked down at the clothes she was wearing.

'Dressed for the occasion, then? I can hardly recognise you without your flowery wellington boots, Alice!'

She laughed and they hugged each other. Donald was much taller than Alice, and he planted a kiss on the top of her head.

'Donald, this is my friend Charlie, and this is my sister Lori.'

Charlie shook hands shyly, and Lori sort of dipped in a silly little curtsy. Then Donald turned and grinned at Alice.

'By my recollection, Alice, you're a couple of weeks early. But as far as I'm concerned you arrived on the right day – just in time to meet our new addition, born yesterday! Come on inside.'

Elsa Gillies was clearing away dishes from the table when they stepped into the Fergusons' house. His wife looked quizzically at Donald when she saw the visitors, and dried her hands hastily on her apron. She was a small, neat person with rosy cheeks and dark brown hair. A child tugged at her skirt, and in the corner of the room Alice could see a newborn baby lying fast asleep in a basket. Standing beside the baby was the ornate candlestick that had belonged to Lady Grange, the candle's flame burning bright and steady. Alice stared at it for a moment. She was picturing it back in Lady Grange's cave.

'Congratulations, Elsa. I'm Alice. I knew your husband when he was a boy.' She then realised that must sound strange coming from an eleven-year-old child, so she changed the subject.

'What have you called the baby?'

'He hasn't got a name yet.'

Alice peeped into the basket and stroked the baby's cheek.

'Hello, James,' she said.

'Hmm, I like that, Alice,' murmured Donald. 'James… what do you think, Elsa?'

All at once Alice was aware that whatever she knew about Donald's future – the war, the plane crash, his rescue, James's life – could not be revealed to Donald. She felt certain it was one of the golden rules of being a time-traveller. Instead she should concentrate on what had already happened or was about to happen.

'So you're leaving at the end of this month, is that right?' she enquired. Elsa was making tea in the yellow teapot Alice recognised from James's house.

'Yes, we have arranged to go to Glasgow,' Donald explained. 'The Post Office have offered to relocate me. I'm to be postmaster of a branch on the outskirts of the city.'

'That'll be a massive change for you all, won't it? I've been to Glasgow once – it's a big place,' Alice ventured.

Charlie was playing with Donald's older son and Lori was helping Elsa make up a tray of teacups and a plate of oatcakes.

'You should take it easy,' Lori said to her. 'I can't believe you're up and about if the baby was only born yesterday.'

'I'm OK,' Elsa said, smiling and pouring the tea, but she looked tired.

They all fell silent, and there was just the sound of James's brother pushing a wooden truck along the floor.

'Well drink up, Alice. There are a couple of things I want to show you while you're here. How long are you staying?'

Alice checked her watch. 'Only an hour or so, I'm afraid. We are leaving St Kilda this afternoon…'

She didn't know how much Donald had told Elsa about where she came from, but what with the new baby, his wife seemed to have many more important things on her mind to care. So she added, 'Part of our house burned down in a fire and we have to go and stay with my father's parents in Liverpool while it all gets fixed.'

'I'm sorry to hear that. Did you lose many things?'

Alice shook her head, not wanting to reveal that this tiny baby's precious notebook was amongst the items that had been lost.

'So, what did you want to show us, Donald?' she asked.

'Our tree! It's quite big now – come and see,' he urged, leading them round to the back of the cottage. Alice ran her hands over its leaves, nodding her approval.

'I'm glad you like it, Alice. Let's call in next door now and say hello to Dora. She won't be the only one to be amazed to see you again. There's someone else you know living at her house these days,' Donald said with a mischievous chuckle.

'I can't imagine what you're talking about,' Alice said, already intrigued.

'Don't be long, Alice!' Lori called from the doorway. 'I'm staying here to help Elsa so she can have a rest.' Lori couldn't resist doing the big sister routine.

Dora looked a lot older and thinner but she still wore her hair in a bun. She stared in wonder at Alice and Charlie, rubbing her hands together and peering at the clothes they were wearing.

'I am sure I knitted that cardigan, Alice – where did you get it? Come over here, Charlie. I think I may have also knitted that wee jumper you're wearing.'

She touched the wool and laughed. Another cackle of laughter seemed to be coming from a cloth that was draped over a box in the corner of the room near where Donald was standing. He grinned and with a sudden flick of his wrist he pulled the cloth off the box like a magician.

'Ta-da!' he crooned.

'*Olá!*' croaked another little voice.

Alice stared in amazement at the bright blue parrot as he moved from side to side along the bar in his cage, looking embarrassed.

'Spix!' She was speechless for a moment.

'Parrots live a very long time. He must be getting on for 90, we think.'

'But how on earth ...' Alice's question trailed off as she walked over to the cage to look more closely at the bird.

'I had to go to London on business once in the late 1920s, and while I was there I ran into a funny little man with white curly hair who told me he had a business importing exotic birds and animals. When I told him about a parrot I once knew that spoke in Portuguese, he demanded that I went with him to his shop and there was Spix. I used all the money I had just earned to buy him.'

Alice opened the cage and Spix flew out and perched on her shoulder, croaking '*Muito mau, perigroso!*' and bobbing his head with excitement.

'He's been a good friend to me, but he's yours, Alice,' Dora said firmly, smiling. 'I never thought I'd see you again! You don't look any older, mind.'

Alice stroked the bird's blue feathers. 'Well I'm only a couple of months older than when we first met, that's why.'

'I see. Well in that case I'm not sure whether I should give you the other thing back or not.' Dora opened the lid of a very familiar black sea chest behind her and started sifting through its contents, just as Alice had rummaged in it when she went to clear Jim's house out a week or so before.

'Ah. Here it is. I've forgotten what she called it. Odd-looking thing, like one of those typewriters people have nowadays.'

Dora handed Alice Karla's laptop. Its black casing was slightly warm to the touch.

'I'd forgotten you still had it, Mother,' remarked Donald. 'Karla was obsessed with getting that machine working again. No one believed me when I told them she was stealing things from the Wireless Station – she was after tiny bits of wire and metal – and she fiddled away at it for days. She told me she was making a "solar battery" for it, and then one day she just vanished. They all thought she must have been smuggled off the island one night by the German secret service when she was supposed to be decoding their messages for us.'

Charlie took the laptop from Alice, flipped it open and pressed the power button.

'It's dead, right?' asked Alice.

'Yep. We'd need to figure out how the thermopower battery works if we want to get it going again.'

'It says something on the bottom, a date – look,' Dora said, showing them a small label stuck on the base of the machine.

Alice and Donald were both peering over Charlie's shoulder and said out loud in unison, 'Checked 1 April 2118'. Charlie chuckled.

'Well, someone got that wrong by a century!'

'Unless …' Alice was frowning – something didn't add up here.

'Unless what?' Donald asked her.

'What if Karla didn't arrive on the island from Germany in 2018? We already know she didn't actually work for the firm she said she did, and that Karla Ingermann isn't the name on her passport. What if she's from the future? I mean, from *our* future. Charlie, you said yourself you'd never seen a laptop as advanced as this before. What if she *is* a spy, working for a rival company to whoever made our C-Bean, and they sent her back from the future because they wanted her to work out how to make one just like it? What if that was why she took all those pictures? And what if that C-Bean Mark 4 upgrade we allowed it to perform happened because Karla was making changes to it from the future – I mean trying to sabotage it? Maybe she made its operating system go corrupt, and that's what made the cardkey catch fire!'

Chapter 16: Shutdown

Alice's brain was on overload, wheeling through all the possibilities. Spix kept squawking *'Muito mau, muito mau!'*, as if he could read her mind.

'Slow down, Alice. So what you're saying is that Karla could have summoned the C-Bean back to 1918 remotely using this laptop, in order to get back to her own time?'

'Yes, that's exactly what I'm saying.'

'Well, it would explain the time she went missing in 1918 and also when the C-Bean went missing in 2018. But I still don't get why she would have returned it to us.'

'I've no idea either. But I bet when we get this thing going again there'll be stuff on it that might tell us why.'

They said goodbye and left Dora's house. Donald wanted to take Alice and Charlie on a tour to see the gun emplacement. They both pretended to be surprised when he whispered to them that there was a secret cave underneath.

'It made all the islanders feel a lot safer when that got installed in October 1918, I can tell you, after what happened in May. You never know, the cave might come in useful at some point in your future,' remarked Donald, giving Charlie a wink.

The three of them were sitting on a bench in the sunshine in front of the chapel while Spix flew around in front of them. Although the islanders were familiar with the exotic blue bird, Alice felt a little conspicuous sitting there with Karla's laptop, even though their clothes made them blend in, but people seemed too caught up with their preparations for departure to notice Donald's two companions.

'What will you do when you leave, Donald? I mean with the house.'

'Elsa and the women have talked about it. They plan to lay the table in each house with a freshly-laundered cloth, and leave a candle burning and a bible open at the book of Exodus. It'll be a sad day. People have survived on St Kilda for centuries. It doesn't seem right that we're the generation that's giving up, when our lives are probably much easier compared to those of any of our predecessors. But it's good to know that people come back and live here again eventually, Alice. Knowing that makes all the difference, even if I can't share it with anyone here.'

'What does Elsa know?'

'You don't remember her, do you?'

'No, should I?'

'Elsa was one of my classmates. She was eight when you came in 1918. So she knows where you're from. She was there – she came with us to see the Great Exhibition. Don't you remember that little girl who held your hand?'

'Yes, of course. Elsa.' Alice wasn't thinking about the little girl – instead she was wondering where Elsa had been in 1944, and why James hadn't mentioned her.

'Look, here comes your sister.'

Lori was half walking, half running down the street towards them.

'I really think we should go back now, Alice,' she puffed, a little out of breath.

'OK,' Alice said slowly, feeling in her pocket for the cardkey.

'Where did you leave your Time Machine this time, Alice?' Donald asked.

'It has developed a habit of becoming invisible, remember!' Alice stood up and smoothed her pinafore. 'But you get it back with this,' she said, showing him the cardkey.

They walked down to the schoolyard and Donald and Lori watched in amazement as the C-Bean just materialised in front of them. Donald ran his hands over its smooth walls. The door opened and Spix flew straight in, followed by the three children. Alice lingered in the doorway, not sure what to say.

'Well, goodbye, Donald. I'm glad our elm seed grew, and I can't tell you how happy I am to see Spix again! I haven't got anything to give you this time, sorry. But do me a favour – before you leave St Kilda on the 29th, will you leave me a letter in the secret cave for us?'

'Yes, I'll do that. Will we meet again, Alice?'

'I … have a feeling we might. Look after James for me.'

Alice managed to suppress all the many things she had bottled up inside that could not be said.

✠ ✠ ✠

It took a while before Alice noticed that the laptop she was clutching was getting hotter. It was only when Lori asked why it was so warm inside the C-Bean that Alice realised Karla's laptop was the cause. She put it down on the floor suddenly and examined her fingers – they were burning from holding it.

'Ice, I need ice,' she stammered and a bucket of cubes appeared in a recess.

'Lori, don't just stand there – can you pass it to me!'

In a state of shock at the C-Bean's powers, Lori finally responded and Alice plunged both hands into the ice.

'We need to get back quickly. This thing's overheating for some reason.'

They were all sweating. Lori took a cube of ice and rolled it over her forehead. Spix had spread out his wings and was lying awkwardly on the floor. Charlie took off his sweater, knelt down and gingerly opened the laptop using the sweater like an oven mitt.

'Look! It's started working again. Maybe it's overheating because it's trying to charge itself using C-Bean's thermopower!'

He nudged the laptop round with his elbow to face the two girls. The screen displayed a red dialogue box that blinked the question 'Allow remote override function?'

'No way! That proves we were right about one thing,' Alice said grimly.

'You really think Karla is trying to control it again now?' Charlie asked incredulously.

'Impossible to say for sure. We just have to try and beat her to it. St Kilda schoolyard, 4th August 2018, NOW!' barked Alice, her face sweaty and her eyes shining.

The C-Bean did not respond. The heat was getting unbearable. Then the same red dialogue box appeared on the wall beside them, and below it was another box into which someone with the username KROB2090 was typing. They watched as a sentence formed itself, the words blinding white against black:

'Product Recall by order of Hadron Services Ltd. C-Bean Mark 4 total system shutdown scheduled 12.00 hours, 04/08/2018.'

Alice looked at her watch. It was 11.45. She felt her stomach clench up.

'Charlie – the shutdown's happening in fifteen minutes!'

'What's going on, Alice? What are you talking about?' Lori wailed.

'*Perigroso!*' squawked Spix in a high-pitched voice.

'*Hadron*. I know that name from somewhere,' Alice wondered out loud, ignoring her sister. She screwed up her eyes. She pictured the name written in a crazy scrawl of fiery reds and yellows. Then she remembered it was in New York when they came back to Central Park and found the C-Bean with graffiti all over it. 'Hadron burn in hell!', someone had written.

'Alice, you need to do something to stop the shutdown from happening! Whoever KROB2090 is, they're trying to ground us for some reason,' Charlie urged in a panicky voice.

'Yes, but why?'

'I don't know. But I don't want to be stuck in here for the rest of my life! Think!'

'Alice, this is all your fault,' Lori blurted tearfully. 'I can't believe this is happening!'

'Get a grip, Lori! I'll figure it out if you can both just be quiet.'

They all fell silent. Alice sat down cross-legged on the floor, and Spix settled next to her. She stroked his feathers and closed her eyes. Flowing through her mind were images of the time she was diverted away from the War Office men in 1957, when the C-Bean took her back to Lady Grange's time. But they were somehow mixed up with James's prototype C-Bean, which they'd found in the secret chamber. It was as if she had no control over her own memories, as if the C-Bean was sifting through its own database using her brain. She forced her mind back to the first time she was stuck inside it with Karla when they ended up in 1918 by accident.

'I've got it!'

She opened her eyes. Playing over all the walls like a silent movie were all the events she'd just been recalling, like a visual log of her activities over the last few months, including the day Alice and Karla were arrested in 1918, and the terrible night she rescued Donald in 1944. Lori was watching with a look of awe and horror on her face.

'Alice, what have you been through?'

'Charlie, remember how we did a factory reset back in May?'

'Yeah, but you ended up a hundred years ago, remember. I want to land in the present, thank you.'

'What if this time we reset it to a date that's ever so slightly into the future?'

'Can you even do that?'

'We've got to be back in time to catch the ferry, remember! To our *real life*,' Lori pointed out impatiently.

'OK – I don't know if it will work, but here's the plan. We reset the C-Bean to 11.50 tomorrow, which is about the time we were due to get there anyway if we'd gone by ferry and train. We'll text Mum and Dad to say we'll meet them there.'

'They'll never believe that story,' Lori argued.

'But will it actually stop the shutdown?'

'I don't know, Charlie, but it will buy us a bit more time while KROB2090 figures out some other way of recalling the C-Bean.'

'You can't do this, Alice!' Lori was dripping with sweat.

'Lori, we've got no choice. It's our only option. Unless you want to be stranded in 1930 for ever! I promise when we get to Liverpool we'll tell Mum and Dad everything. Deal?'

Lori sighed and nodded meekly.

'Ready, Charlie? Let's give it a try. Charlie – before we do this, can you use your mobile and send a quick text to my parents, and one to yours too. Then switch it off.'

'Right, I'm on it.'

Alice cleared her throat.

'Pen!' she commanded, wanting to issue the command accurately.

Consulting her watch, she picked up the pen and wrote slowly and deliberately on the wall, 'Liverpool, England, 05/08/2018, 11.55.'

'Wait up! I'm not arriving in Liverpool wearing this ridiculous outfit. You've got to tell this thing to get me something different to wear.'

Alice rolled her eyes and stopped writing.

'We haven't exactly got much time left Lori, but OK, new clothes all round!'

A recess opened up in the wall behind Charlie like a mini wardrobe containing three new outfits on hangers. Alice smirked.

'I think the fluorescent one's yours, Lori,' she said as she checked her watch again and updated the time code to 11.58 and added the final full stop to her command line.

Lori was just about to change when the C-Bean seemed to jerk violently, there were some weird flashes, and the interior was then plunged into darkness. There was a strange booming sound coming from outside the C-Bean.

Charlie cleared his throat.

'Do you think it worked?'

'I sincerely hope so. Did the texts send?' Alice asked anxiously. Charlie turned his phone back on to check.

'Apparently, yes.'

'Well, let's get changed and try to get out of here.'

They all fumbled around in the dark trying to work out which outfit was which, discarding their 1930s clothes on the floor.

'Hey Alice, look!' Charlie whispered, doing his belt up.

'What is it?' Lori asked.

To Alice's utter amazement and relief, a new dialogue box had appeared on the wall, and across it flowed the words:

... Reset complete. Remote override function cancelled. Timeline temporarily revised by system administrator. Timeline reverting in 3 minutes ...

'I don't know exactly what that means, but I think we should get out of here before it reverts back to being yesterday,' Alice said, opening the door to a blast of summer heat coming off the concrete in front of her. Spix burst out, his blue feathers merging with the clear blue sky overhead.

For some reason, the C-Bean had decided to arrive with its cargo of children at the new Liverpool Passenger Terminal, just as a vast white cruise ship moved out into the Mersey. The booming sound was the cruise ship's foghorn announcing its departure for the Caribbean. Hundreds of passengers stood on deck waving goodbye to their families and friends who lined the dockside. No one seemed to pay any attention to the C-Bean – perhaps they thought this black cube was nothing more than a buoy that had come loose from its moorings, floated across the sea and been randomly washed up here, like an enormous seabean.

No one, that is, except a man with curly white hair who stood out from the crowd because he reminded Alice of her old teacher Dr Foster. As Alice stepped out of the C-Bean and removed the cardkey from its slot, she noticed the man turn to look at her and begin to edge away from the crowd of people. He was carrying a battered leather suitcase and walking purposefully towards them.

'Come on Alice, we've got to go,' Lori said, pulling her sister in the opposite direction. 'Mum and Dad and Kit will be arriving at the train station in about twenty minutes. Let's be there to meet them.'

But Alice hung back as the man approached. She noticed he was waving to get their attention.

'Charlie, look – isn't that Dr Foster?'

The man had broken into a trot in an effort to catch up with them. Alice could hear his knee clicking as he got closer.

'Alice, wait, I need to talk to you!' he panted. 'There's something wrong with the C-Bean! Come, let me tell you about Plan B before it's too late.'

Alice stiffened.

It really was their teacher, Dr Foster, but there was something odd about the way he spoke – for some reason his voice sounded as if it was computer-generated. Wondering how to respond, she glanced at her watch and stuffed the cardkey nervously in her pocket, when Spix suddenly let out a loud cry and started to chase Dr Foster, who was now running along the dockside towards the C-Bean. Alice noticed that the black cube was starting to wobble and flicker. She watched in astonishment as it slowly changed into a shimmering golden object in the heat. Since everything seemed to be happening in slow motion, it occurred to her that perhaps the dazzling gold C-Bean was only a mirage created by the heat. But before Alice even had a chance to say anything to the others, Dr Foster, the parrot and the C-Bean merged into one luminous thing and then slowly vanished.

Alice shook her head and blinked, her eyes fixed on the spot they had just vacated, as if willing them back into existence, but it was now nothing more than a bright afterimage that remained even when she closed her eyes. She was aware that Charlie and Lori were both calling her to come, but she was somehow unable to move. She could feel the warm sun on her eyelids and a strange dizziness came over her. Surging out of the centre of the glowing afterimage in quick succession was a steady flow of familiar faces from her immediate past: Karla Ingermann, Donald, James and Dora Ferguson, Lady Grange in her long blue dress, and lastly, rushing towards her and barking like mad, Spex. The barking didn't stop until Alice opened her eyes and saw the little brown dog was running in circles around her feet, his tail wagging, and a brand new collar and lead around his neck. Alice felt the dizziness pass and crouched down to stroke him. She noticed that his fur was going grey around his muzzle and he was limping slightly.

'Spex, where on earth did you come from? Is it really you? Come here little fellow,' Alice ruffled the wiry fur on his back.

'You poor thing. You look so old!'

There was some kind of tag attached to Spex's collar. Alice held it up in the sunlight, expecting it to be Donald's Second World War dogtag. But it wasn't. It was a heavy gold disc the size of a two pound coin which was coated black on one side. Engraved on the black side it said *Øbsidon 0902*, and on the reverse was the name 'Børk'.

'Did they give you a new name, Spex?' Alice asked, taking hold of the lead. 'Never mind, you're still our old Spex, come on, let's go and meet Granny and Gramps and the rest of the Robertsons.'

Reading Guide to SeaWAR
Suggestions for class/reading group discussions

1. This story deals with several different time periods in history. Why do you think each one has been selected?

2. How is the character of Karla Ingermann presented and developed in the story and what do the other characters make of her?

3. Can you give an account of what happens between 1918 and 1944 from Donald's perspective?

4. What do you imagine James Ferguson knows about Alice and her time travel machine before he meets her?

5. What is James concerned is happening on the island of St Kilda and how is he investigating matters?

6. Alice faces many challenges in this story, what in your view are the key moments where she puts two and two together and works out something really important?

7. How does the relationship between Alice and her sister Lori change over the course of SeaWAR and what causes this to happen?

8. How does the story deal with people's different reactions to illness, injury, death and loss?

9. What happens to Lady Grange after she arrives back in 2018 with Alice? Can you write an account from her point of view?

10. There is evidence of spying and subterfuge in SeaWAR: how does this impact directly on the development of the story?

11. Describe the life that people lead on St Kilda in the early twentieth century and say why you think they found it necessary to evacuate in 1930.

12. The C-Bean makes several appearances and disappearances throughout the story – who do you think is controlling it at different points, how are they doing it and why?

A PREVIEW OF

SeaRISE

Book III of the
SeaBEAN Trilogy

SARAH HOLDING

It's the year 2118: Alice and her schoolmates find they
have been summoned to the future in the C-Bean and
imprisoned there by its inventor. Realising they must
now know too much, yet trapped in a world they no
longer understand, they have to plan an escape route
back to the present before it's too late and the planet
is ruined forever.

SeaRISE

SARAH HOLDING

The light inside Alice's globe beside her bed grew brighter and brighter until she half opened her eyes. It was better than an alarm clock as a way of waking up, and besides it was her secret reminder of all the places she'd been around the world. Alice scrunched up her pillow and half sat up in bed. She could hear her parents moving around in the kitchen, the clatter of things being put out for Saturday morning breakfast, the odd gurgle from her baby brother Kit, Spex pushing his dog bowl around the flagged floor as he licked it clean.

Alice wriggled in the warmth under her duvet and stared up at the glow-in-the-dark stars on her ceiling. It felt good to have her old bedroom back exactly how it used to be before the fire. And it was good to be back on St Kilda after staying with her grandparents in Liverpool, even if it was the end of the summer holidays now. School was starting again on Monday: her last year at their tiny island primary school of six children before she could join her sister Lori at high school on the mainland. Alice was even glad to have her mother back as their teacher again. 2018 had felt very disjointed so far, what with the arrival of baby Kit, and the arrival and departure of Dr Foster, their replacement teacher, followed by the appearance and suspicious disappearance of Karla Ingermann, the C-Bean's designer, quite apart from all the crazy comings and goings they'd had in the C-Bean itself. The only person still left from all their time travel adventures was Lady Grange – or rather Rachel Chiesley, as she was now called – who decided to stay on St Kilda when they asked her if she would like to be the new teaching assistant.

It made Alice feel dizzy just thinking about everything that had happened since in the last eight months, and she had already decided that in this school year the past would remain in the past. Alice herself would remain in the present and wait impatiently for her future to begin, just like any other normal 11-year-old kid. Anyway, now that the adults knew about the C-Bean's time travel function, it was useless thinking they would have any further adventures in their 'rather too mobile classroom', as her dad put it. Her mum – that is to say Mrs Robertson – had been required to write a full report for the Hebridean School Board about what had taken place when Alice, Charlie and Lori vanished the morning they were supposed to leave by ferry for Oban, and then just turned up in Liverpool the next day, apparently in the C-Bean. Alice could scarcely imagine how her mother had explained this particular event, and was grateful for her mum's sake that not everything had come to light: as Alice saw it, apart from James and Donald, it was beyond any adult's imagination to grasp the full extent of their time travels.

'Alice, are you getting up now? Breakfast is ready,' her mother called.

'In a minute!' she called, sliding her feet sideways out of bed to land on the orange shaggy rug. She threw back the duvet, stood up and shuddered just like Spex when he was shaking off water. Then she took a deep breath, opened the drawer of her bedside cabinet and took out the C-Bean's Mark 3 cardkey, James' red notebook and the photo of his christening, together with his letters and Donald's sheaf of memoirs. Alice knew that although these things all meant a lot to her, they were a strange burden she'd been carrying. Even the things that no longer existed still weighed heavy: the other older brown notebook that had belonged to James and the Mark 4 cardkey, that had both been destroyed when their house caught fire. This was all that was left.

'Time to move on,' she murmured to herself, pulling an old shoebox from under her bed. She emptied out the random assortment of toys, birthday cards and dead batteries, and placed her historic items inside in a neat pile. She put the lid back on and, using a black felt-tip pen, she wrote in capitals on the lid of the box:

**1st SEPTEMBER 2018
TIME CAPSULE OF ALICE ROBERTSON**

It would need a better box, she decided, but she already knew where it should be left: in the secret chamber under the gun emplacement. She slid the box back under the bed, and decided she would perform the ceremony with her schoolmates Edie and Charlie after their first day back at school on Monday.

✠ ✠ ✠

Early that Monday morning, Alice pushed Kit's buggy slowly down the main street of the Village towards down to the Burney's house with Spex running on ahead, thinking he was being taken for a walk. Edie Burney's mother was going to take care of him and Kit during the day from now on, so that Alice's mother could teach the children again.

'Spex, sit. Good boy.' She patted his head, but he looked bitterly disappointed that his walk had already come to an abrupt end. Alice had an odd feeling as she knocked on the Burney's door, which back in the twentieth century had been Dora's house. Alice's dad once told her this feeling when you think you've done something exactly the same before was called '*déjà-vu*' – he reckoned that although it *feels* as if something's already happened, it's just your brain playing tricks on you. Except this was real *déjà-vu* – she *had* knocked on this very same door in 1930, just a couple of weeks earlier. Alice had her eyes half closed when the door opened. Spex slunk inside, tail between his legs. Edie's mum smiled and lifted Kit out of the buggy.

'Come here my little lamb! Alice, run along now, you'll be late. You look like you're not quite awake yet sweetheart . . . did you eat enough breakfast?'

'I'm fine thanks, I was just remembering something,' Alice said, turning to leave, one half of her still in 1930. The last time she had walked away from this house was with Donald, carrying Karla's confiscated laptop which had been in Dora's possession since 1918. Although Charlie had got it working again, they still hadn't managed to crack Karla's username and password, which was frustrating because they both knew whatever was stored on that machine might explain a lot of things.

Alice ran the rest of the way to school, her heart pumping. Counting footsteps was the last thing on her mind, all she could see were hundreds of lines of computer code.

✠ ✠ ✠

The class was sitting in silence when she arrived and there was a tense atmosphere. Alice slid into her seat and darted a quick look at Charlie. He raised his eyebrows in a mock question and nodded towards their teacher, who was engrossed in reading a letter. It had evidently just arrived, since Mr Butterfield was hovering at her elbow as if expecting Mrs Robertson to write an instant reply for him to deliver by return. Alice peered at the papers on her mother's desk, and spied an envelope with a spinning globe holographic logo on it. It could only mean one thing: Karla. Even to this day, no one had any idea how or why she'd vanished.

Mrs Robertson cleared her throat and looked up to address the class. Six pairs of eyes were trained on her face.

'OK kids, this is how it is. Sorry to be the bearer of bad news, especially on our first day back. Our C-Bean has, as you know, caused some concern among the authorities, and it seems that this has escalated to a very high level now, with the Ministry of Defence getting involved for some reason. The German company that manufactures these education pods contacted the Hebridean School Board to say they need to recall the C-Bean for a complete refit, but I've also received another more serious letter from a Scottish government official, who intends to visit the island this week, apparently to impound the C-Bean and carry out a full inquiry. They say 'suspicious circumstances' have been brought to their attention, and now they want "our complete co-operation", although I don't know what that means exactly.'

Alice could see the two Sams were simmering with fury and confusion. They kept looking out of the window at the three-metre wide black cube that was their C-Bean, standing innocently in the schoolyard, and then back at each other. In the end, they could not contain themselves.

'But they can't take it away, it's ours!' Sam F blurted out.

'Yes, that's not fair Mrs Robertson, it was a present!' chimed Sam J.

'I know, I know, but I don't think they will let us keep it, boys, I'm sorry. Not now. Not after what's happened.'

Alice felt sure that the suspicious circumstances they'd mentioned had nothing to do with the excursion to Liverpool, and would probably have more to do with Karla disappearing and not being who she said she was and who knows what else, but Alice decided to say nothing until she'd talked to Charlie at break. The only thing she felt sure about was that it would be better if the Scottish government took it away than if the company Karla was working for were to get it back from them. That is, if it really did belong to Karla's company.

Edie put up her hand: 'Can we still have lessons in the C-Bean until it's taken away, Mrs Robertson?'

'I'm not sure, it doesn't say anywhere here that we shouldn't use it…' Mrs Robertson's voice trailed off, uncertain. Charlie had the look of someone with a light bulb switching on above their head.

'Well if it's going to be taken away from us, we should at least have a final goodbye celebration: how about we have a sleepover in it, like they do at the Science Museum in London sometimes, you know, with our sleeping bags?' he suggested casually, but Alice could hear the sense of urgency in his voice – she'd heard it before.

Mrs Robertson glanced up at Mr Butterfield, then at Lady Grange who was sharpening pencils beside her, and shrugged her shoulders.

'Great idea, why not Charlie. You can all do that on Friday evening if you like. Now let's get on with some work shall we?'

Mr Butterfield tugged one end of his moustache for a moment, and then said, 'Right, that's sorted then, I'll be off then Jen, got to do my "mailboat" duties.'

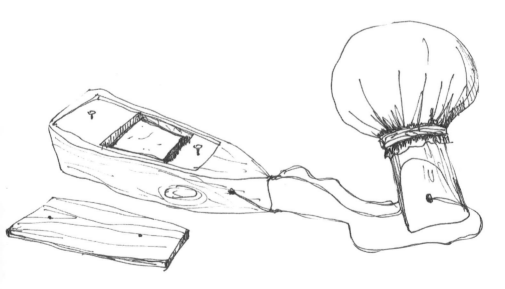

'Mailboat,' Alice murmured, picturing all those messages people used to send in the olden days from St Kilda in strange little homemade packages, all sealed up to float across the sea like messages in a bottle, hoping for food, medicine or salvation. She thought about how she'd sent her own messages back and forth in time to James using his homemade 'instant mailboat' drawer invention on his prototype C-Bean. If only she could send some kind of mailboat now, to appeal for the C-Bean's salvation, or at the very least to stop it from being taken away.

How does the cover of the SeaBEAN book reveal an image when touched?

The covers of the SeaBEAN Trilogy are printed like a normal book, but another very special ink is then printed on top. This special ink is called a leuco dye and is thermochromic, which means it changes its appearance when the temperature changes.

SeaBEAN has been printed with a black leuco dye that goes from black to clear at just under 37 degrees Celsius (which is normal body temperature). The dye is composed of pigment particles with a solvent that melts at a certain temperature. When the cover is warm from the body heat from your hand – or your teacup, or the sun – the solvent is in its melted form and the pigment particles don't join with each other, allowing you to see through to the picture behind. When the book cover is cold the solvent is solid and the lueco dye particles join together to form a black coating so you can't see what is underneath.

Visit http://www.colorchange.com/leuco-dyes

What readers say about the SeaBEAN Trilogy

"This book was gripping, capturing, unputdownable and awesome! It was also an exciting and imaginative book. I found out lots of facts about the environment."

The Guardian

"I am giving SeaBEAN to my 8-year-old twin grandchildren to read… they are going to be captivated by the hero of the story, 11-year-old Alice."

Huffington Post

"There's no feeling that you are reading a children's book, as the language is clear and intelligent - and yet you are drawn into a dream-like state where impossible events seem perfectly reasonable. Highly recommended."

GoodReads

"An absorbing and intelligent tale with a strong environmental angle."

The Swallow's Nest

"Told with a mixture of faux blog postings and conventional narrative, SeaBEAN is an enjoyable fantasy with a clear message about environmental stewardship."

Joe Follansbee

'Flawlessly written, the language is simple and straightforward but not condescending for young readers... the pace romps along with constant changes of venue and lots of adventure."

Best Book Review

"It is the best book that I have read..... EVER, and I can't wait for the next book in the series. It is perfect for ages 9+.'

Mia, age 10

 Visit The SeaBEAN Trilogy site

 Visit the author's Facebook page

 Visit Medina Publishing Ltd

Teddington School Library